THE *Second* SEASON

HEATHER CHAPMAN

SWEETWATER
BOOKS
An imprint of Cedar Fort, Inc.
Springville, Utah

This is a work of fiction. The characters, names, incidents, places, and dialogue are products of the author's imagination and are not to be construed as real. The opinions and views expressed herein belong solely to the author and do not necessarily represent the opinions or views of Cedar Fort, Inc. Permission for the use of sources, graphics, and photos is also solely the responsibility of the author.

ISBN 13: 978-1-4621-1884-7

Published by Sweetwater Books, an imprint of Cedar Fort, Inc., 2373 W. 700 S., Springville, UT 84663
Distributed by Cedar Fort, Inc. www.cedarfort.com

LIBRARY OF CONGRESS CATALOGING-IN-PUBLICATION DATA

Names: Chapman, Heather, 1986- author.
Title: The second season / Heather Chapman.
Description: Springville, Utah : Sweetwater Books, an imprint of Cedar Fort, Inc., [2016]
Identifiers: LCCN 2016012542 | ISBN 9781462118847 (pbk.)
Subjects: LCSH: Social classes--Fiction. | Young women--Fiction. | Courtship--Fiction. | Mate selection--Fiction. | GSAFD: Regency fiction. | LCGFT: Romance fiction. | Domestic fiction.
Classification: LCC PS3603.H369 S43 2016 | DDC 813/.6--dc23
LC record available at http://lccn.loc.gov/2016012542

Cover design by Michelle May Ledezma

Edited and typeset by Jessica Romrell

Printed in the United States of America

10 9 8 7 6 5 4 3 2 1

Printed on acid-free paper

To Mom, for always being in my corner,
and to my girls, I'll always be in yours.

"With characters calling to mind the March girls and society adventures worthy of Frances Burney, this is a genuine and thoughtful treatment of young love and its reasons."

-Kaki Olsen, author of *Swan and Shadow: A Swan Lake Story*

"A sweet romance that will keep you reading. You'll be rooting for the headstrong heroine from beginning to end."

-Tracy Winegar, author of *Good Ground* and The Counterfeit Series

"A fun debut with characters that will capture your heart."

-Tara Mayoros, author of *Broken Smiles, Eight Birds for Christmas,* and *The Christmas Bike*

"A delightful read and charmingly told, I found myself lost in this regency-era love story. It was hard to put down and left me guessing up until its last pages!"

-Lindsay B. Ferguson, author of *By the Stars*

"The Second Season is a sweet, lighthearted Regency-set romance that gives you more than one happy ending to root for!"

-Dantzel Cherry, author of *Miss Darcy's First Intergalactic Ballet Class* and *The Price of Love*

CHAPTER 1

Eleanor turned her head at the sight of Mr. Cranston. He was stroking his mustache with a wet finger as he stared down at her. She had not addressed him directly all evening, but still his gaze would not leave her. It was only her first season, and Eleanor did not yet know how to dissuade the attentions of an unwanted suitor.

Mr. Cranston had moved closer. He was discussing his displeasure of dancing again. Each time the man smiled, a maze of wrinkles instantaneously appeared across his face. His eyes, once considered fine by many a lady, were now dimmed by his forty-eight years, specifically the thirty years of drinking and emptiness that had filled them.

It was no use. Try as she might, Eleanor could not shake off her feelings of disappointment. It had only been two months ago that she had met Phillip in this very room. It had been a dark evening, much like this one, and he had come late. He had stood at the door, offering a greeting to the host, when she had caught his eyes falling upon her. His tall frame trembled as he nodded gently at her. It was then that Eleanor knew her heart was lost. She felt it in an instant. In the months that followed, Phillip Hopkins had not let even two days pass without seeing her. That was, until two weeks ago.

Eleanor had gone to town daily in hopes of meeting him. She attended every invitation and ball without success. She began to think Phillip neglectful, or far worse, blind to her regard for him. After much deliberation, she had written to him personally, asking for his presence at the party this evening. Her letter had gone unanswered.

"—which is why I am always so disgusted by such displays. Dancing around the room like a pair of peacocks," Mr. Cranston was saying. "Call me old fashioned if you like, but I am of the opinion that a lady should not be objected to such lunacy. Surely Miss Davenport agrees with me, hmm?"

The sound of her name startled her. She turned toward Mr. Cranston and raised her small hand in protest. "Mr. Cranston, you must excuse me. I find I am unforgivably distracted."

Mr. Cranston furrowed his brow. "Miss Davenport, are you all right?"

Eleanor nodded, standing up from the soft chair. "I am only in need of fresh air."

"Please, allow me to be of assistance," he whispered in reply. His breathing had quickened, and he now towered over her. His eyes stared down at her in keen anticipation.

Eleanor instinctively stepped backward in repulsion, but the man was by no means discouraged. She deliberated for a moment but determined to accept his outstretched arm. Phillip had not come, and Eleanor began to feel she could not wait upon him any longer.

Mr. Cranston had nearly led Eleanor across the room's long expanse when she heard an eruption of excitement. She did not have to turn around to know that Phillip had arrived. Only one man could cause such an uproar.

"Miss Davenport! Miss Davenport, I have been detained," Phillip exclaimed as he made his way toward her.

The company became hushed as he paraded across the room. The elegant Phillip now stood but a few feet from Cranston's side. His dark hair was disheveled from the apparent rush he had taken. His cravat hung loosely and awkwardly around his handsome neck. His green eyes were pleading, begging, and full of hope.

Eleanor stood motionless, her embarrassment heightened by her reddening cheeks. She could not meet his gaze. She nodded modestly and attempted a small smile, but she could not find an appropriate escape from the man in possession of her arm.

Mr. Cranston, for his part, stood stubbornly and did not even acknowledge Phillip. He gave a slight huff at their meeting and uttered a bored and possessive, "Come, Miss Davenport, you are in need of fresh air."

Eleanor helplessly followed, stealing a desperate glance at Phillip.

Phillip stood abandoned at the open door. He was suddenly aware of the many eyes watching him. He turned, forcing himself to smile broadly. The most eligible ladies and bachelors filled the room. Most laughed at seeing Phillip make such a spectacle of himself. Others stared in confusion. But Phillip did not care what anyone thought. He never had. He chuckled to himself as his fingers combed through his hair. Satisfied he had regained his composure, Phillip strolled to the terrace in search of Eleanor.

Poor Eleanor.

She looked positively charming, a fact that had apparently caught the attention of the wealthy but boorish Cranston as well. It was painful to see Eleanor so uncomfortable. Phillip determined he could not help but rescue her. He filed between the small clusters of couples. It was not difficult to find Eleanor, for Cranston had led her to the southernmost side, leaving a large gap between the pair and the rest of the company.

Phillip cleared his throat loudly, attracting the attention of both Eleanor and Cranston. Phillip then raised his voice as he impulsively announced, "Mr. Cranston, I am sorry to inform you that you are wanted at the card table."

Cranston's eyes lowered in irritation. "I do not think you are sorry in the least, Hopkins."

A chuckle escaped Phillip's mouth. He cleared his throat once more. "Mr. Cranston, *I* am not sorry. I simply meant that I was sorry to be the one to inform you. Clearly, you have been favored with the prettiest lady here. No, I am not sorry at all. Nor do I envy the card table at the moment."

Cranston silently eyed Phillip for some time. When it was made clear Phillip was insistent, Cranston stood and turned, huffing as he stormed away.

It wasn't until the old bachelor was out of sight that Phillip had the nerve to steal Eleanor's hand in his. She jerked backward in response, attempting to free herself of his grip. However, the shock on Eleanor's face only encouraged him.

Phillip laughed mischievously and whispered quietly, "Perhaps we are in need of more privacy." He quietly pulled her toward the steps leading to the gardens. Though she shook her head in protest, Eleanor did nothing else to resist his efforts.

Safely hidden in the dark trees, lighted only by the moon, Phillip commenced laughing as he secured Eleanor around the waist.

"Phillip Hopkins! You have been mistaken if you've presumed I am *that* type of lady," she exclaimed. She tried with all her might to escape his embrace, but with each struggle he only tightened his grip.

"Am I mistaken indeed? You wish to marry that old buffoon, eh? I had thought you cared for a younger, more attractive gentleman," he teased, leaning close to her face.

Eleanor fell silent.

Phillip was no longer smiling. He stood, tall as he was, leaning over her, peering seriously in her eyes. "Please," he softly pled, "Will you give me your promise?"

He waited until she met his gaze at last. Her eyes were wet, and Phillip instinctively wiped a tear from her cheek.

"Oh, Phillip," Eleanor answered, "You have had my heart since the moment we met."

Before she could say another word, Phillip scooped her up in an enormously inappropriate kiss.

CHAPTER 2

Twenty-Five Years Later, 1817

Lady Hopkins was fully aware of her exceptional skills as mistress of Whitefield Hall. Within her twenty-four years as the lady of the house, she had transformed Phillip's estate, while also restoring the family's reputation. Though the Hopkins family had always been well established among London followers, a difficulty arose by the hand of the late Lord Whitison Hopkins, baron of Chelmsford. His careless gambling and scandalous behavior almost entirely ruined his nephew Phillip's chances of ever having the estate to call home.

Lady Hopkins, then only Miss Eleanor Davenport, had been just the fix for Phillip's dire circumstances. She had not known of his financial situation when they wed. She had only known that Phillip had been everything fashionable—even the manner in which he walked, his careful compliments, and the handsome smile that had seemed only to belong to her. In short, Miss Eleanor Davenport had been smitten. And at the age of only eighteen, her heart could not be ignored.

Lady Hopkins had been considered a renowned beauty. Nearly half of the eligible bachelors at the time had attempted to court her. Her fortune was almost unheard of, at £60,000 upon her marriage. This fact had miraculously spread throughout London in a matter of days prior to the arrival of her first season. Surprisingly, the only thing more alluring than Lady Hopkins's fortune had been Lady Hopkins herself. Her lustrous dark hair, straight teeth, and hazel eyes were enough to render even the most cynical of men speechless. She had had her pick of suitors.

Lord Hopkins was an attentive husband. He allowed her to assist in managing the estate. It was, after all, Lady Hopkins's thrift and grand fortune that had established the family estate as one of the most envied plots in all of Essex. The estate, though small in comparison with some, was indeed beautiful. Situated only a few miles outside of Chelmsford, Whitefield Hall overlooked beautiful gardens of green, mature trees, and fields of white flowers. The gardens surrounding the great house were always manicured to perfection; assortments of flowers bloomed from the first hint of spring until the frost of fall, and mature trees were seemingly placed to offer the best shade on bright summer days. The house itself had been in the Hopkins family for three generations. The stone structure towered over the green landscape, boasting four floors and nine chimney stacks. The green ivy that climbed the outer walls seemed to only add to the charm the rest of the house and gardens so clearly radiated.

Of course, Lady Hopkins spent the majority of the season in London. Whitefield Hall was only a day ride from London, and the proximity allowed her long visits and all the staff she could want in town. The Hopkins's town home was conveniently placed in a fashionable part of town. The house itself was in Mayfair, bordering Hyde Park. One could access the city pleasures quite easily, while yet feeling a sense of serenity from the noise of the horses and the chatter of the town. And while Lady Hopkins entertained quite often, she was grateful to escape the noise. Her nerves were not what they used to be. Perhaps it was due to the burden of raising her three children. Even with the best governesses and teachers England had to offer, Lady Hopkins still felt it her personal duty to raise her two daughters and heir to their respective ranks.

Lady Hopkins had spent far too much time in disappointment over Phillip John. Her son, known by his second name, John, was the sole heir to the estate and title. While John tried to improve himself, he proved to be a dull sort of boy. He struggled in his history and arithmetic lessons (thank goodness he had not been prone to gamble). At least Lady Hopkins had given him the advantage of becoming a great horseman. The true difficulty was that John had grown to be too much like his father in manners. He had not shown the slightest regard for rank or reputation. There was still hope, however, for John was a mere fifteen years old, but Lady Hopkins had little expectation of him amounting to anything impressive. Unless, Lady Hopkins had thought many times, she could arrange a match with a young lady of unusual skill and popularity. And, perhaps John would someday grow to be more like Lord Hopkins in looks. Maybe then John would trick a lady worth catching into marrying him.

It was the girls that showed promise. Lucy, age twenty, was supremely elegant. She resembled Lady Hopkins with hazel eyes and full lips, though Lucy's hair was a few shades lighter than Lady Hopkins's dark hair. Lucy had dazzled nearly all the men in Chelmsford, a fact that Lady Hopkins took great pride in. Perhaps the greatest credit to Lucy was her kind temperament. She was gracious. She seemed incapable of crossing her mother or father, and she was grateful whenever she was given the chance to assist others. This fact endeared Lucy to almost all she came in contact with. And yet, Lucy had the tendency of leaning too much on her mother's influence. She was ruled all too easily. And while Lady Hopkins gloried in her ability to persuade the girl, Lady Hopkins could not help wishing Lucy showed more individuality. Still, Lucy would make an advantageous match. She had been out two seasons and had already secured multiple offers of marriage, though none were deemed acceptable to Lady Hopkins.

Caroline was Lady Hopkins's particular favorite, a fact that puzzled Lady Hopkins exceedingly, for Caroline seemed to be on a constant crusade to provoke Lady Hopkins. Caroline was a tease, and at times, uncommonly open and honest. She never went so far as to be indecorous, but Caroline was by no means the typical reserved young lady. Her pale skin paired with her dark hair and green eyes was simply breathtaking. Caroline resembled her father in all the right ways. More impressive to Lady Hopkins, however, was Caroline's character. She knew her own mind. At times it did so irritate Lady Hopkins that she could not persuade her younger daughter, but Lady Hopkins still felt Caroline's determination invaluable. Though manners and gentility were the standard of all well-bred ladies, Lady Hopkins also knew the benefits of a lively and original soul. She had the highest hopes for Caroline.

And so it was that Lady Hopkins sent her youngest son off from holiday to school once more with little more than a kiss and a list of commands, informed her daughters of her great matrimonial schemes, and instructed the staff of the impending stay in London. She did not fear failure, for after all her faults, she was sure of this: Lucy and Caroline would be the talk of all London.

Chapter 3

Caroline pressed her hand against the cold glass. The glass began to fog, and she peered at the frost covered hills below her. She traced the windowpane with her finger, wishing she could stay at Whitefield Hall instead of travel to London. As she stared blankly at the ground below, a cascade of memories came pouring into her mind. If everything went according to her mother's plan, Caroline would be married this year. To whom, she did not know.

The trunk hit the floor with great force, pulling Caroline's attention away from the window. Her maid, Louisa, was bent gathering the spilled contents. Caroline watched distractedly.

"Miss Caroline, your trunk is nearly ready," the maid chimed. She sensed the silence and added, "Are you all right? You look rather melancholy."

Caroline gave a slight sigh, and openly acknowledged, "I am feeling down, Louisa. I fear I will miss Whitefield Hall more than I can bear. Mother is determined we shall have a great season, but I am not so convinced."

Louisa stood from the trunk, placing her hands at her hips. She gave Caroline a stern look, as she usually did before dealing out a reprimand. "Miss Caroline, you've never been one to sulk. Don't start now. Young ladies are all the same—crying one moment and giggling the next. Oh fiddle!" She paused, her face softening. "But London is no Whitefield Hall. I will miss this land and house just as you will."

Louisa returned to her attempts at the trunk, eventually pushing it out of the door for a male servant to attend to. Caroline listened as Louisa marched down the hall, calling for Bentley. Bentley, the butler, always kept tabs on all of the staff, and Louisa was sure to be asking for Henry's assistance. Henry was not only the strongest of the Hopkins' employees, but also the most handsome.

The melancholy mood of the morning lingered with Caroline throughout breakfast and afterward into her morning walk. She had always loved going to town. It was exciting to see the busy city with its many people. Caroline had been presented last season and had enjoyed a few social events before her illness had caused the family great concern. Lucy had remained in town with Lord and Lady Hopkins, but Caroline had spent the rest of the season at home with her Aunt Fanny as a companion. The two had spent the winter and spring in utter contentment. In fact, it seemed as though the rest of the family had returned only too quickly. Caroline had been sad to see Aunt Fanny go, and perhaps even more sad to see Lady Hopkins return. Caroline's mother had returned far too enthusiastically, marked by her strong resolve to condition Caroline for the following year.

Nothing was decided. Perhaps there would not be a match suitable. Lady Hopkins often had more ambitions than reality allowed. Perhaps Caroline would not be able to convince a grown man he was in love with her well enough to offer for her hand. At only eighteen, Caroline did not feel in control of her own future. She had always found happiness in Whitefield Hall, her parents, and Lucy. Even her younger brother, John, was worth missing. Who else would she ever tease so? She smiled as she remembered teaching John to say *mon petit chou* in place of "father." Lord Hopkins had almost choked on his dinner that night when his eight-year-old son had referred to him as "his little cabbage." Consequently, John had not wished to ever study French.

Caroline spied her sister walking briskly toward her, draped in a winter cloak and a distraught countenance. Caroline walked slowly toward her, her boots crunching on the frosted path.

"Oh, Caroline!" Lucy puffed. "How could I have forgotten? I forgot to call on Miss Ellison before our journey tomorrow. She will be offended at the slight. She so wishes to come to town with us."

Caroline smiled. "I'm sure she will understand. With all the preparations, one cannot be required to remember absolutely everything. Even the upturned Miss Ellison must afford you that. After all, you have always shown her much more kindness than she has offered either of us."

Lucy was still catching her breath, and she now rested her hand against Caroline's shoulder, swallowing carefully. The sun was bright for a winter's day, and Lucy had to squint while looking at Caroline. "Perhaps you will help me craft an apology to her for Bentley to post later this afternoon?"

"Perhaps," Caroline replied, but she had answered absentmindedly. Her mind was otherwise engaged. Caroline had not forgotten her mother's excited manner the previous night as she told the girls of the eligible prospects. Lady Hopkins had even made a list of some of the London crowd she wished her daughters to associate with. Lucy had shared her mother's excitement, pinching Caroline's cheek when she had sat back in her chair blankly. Caroline was not surprised by her mother's scheming. Lady Hopkins had always been the type to concoct dramatic plans for attaining what she wanted. Caroline knew it would be no different with her or Lucy, but Caroline had hoped she would have at least one full season before being married off.

"Just think! In but a matter of days we will be back in town. I could die of anticipation. I do miss the symphony and all the concerts. And we must visit Mrs. Privett's dress shop again. The materials were absolutely stunning! I felt as if I were floating in her petticoats. You remember Miss Granger from the social at Barton's? She has promised the fashions are truly magnificent this year."

The sound of Lucy's excitement only brought more seriousness to the whole situation. How could Lucy anticipate the season so? With her mother's grand expectations, it was sure to bring the greatest displeasure to Caroline. "Oh yes, the social events shall take over," Caroline said sadly. "You seem rather excited with all this talk of dresses and social gatherings. Are you not dreading Mama's matrimonial schemes?"

Lucy's smile faded as she nodded, stroking Caroline's back. Lucy cleared her throat, putting her arm around her sister. "Oh, Caroline. I should have guessed you would feel so. London is so engaging. If it were up to me, I would live in the city the whole year. I do not think marriage will be so very different. I am prepared to make a match, for I am twenty; though I suppose it would be dull if the gentleman in mind were so very boring or homely. I would not like to be married to an old man either." Lucy stifled a small giggle.

Caroline laughed at this, imagining Lucy as a stepmother to four grown children. Perhaps it would be advantageous to remember the humor in all of this. "I am sure you will find the oldest of bachelors." Caroline teased.

To this, Lucy shook her head vengefully and threatened, "And you shall not even have half an offer!"

Caroline's laughter turned into a calm smile. "At least you will be there with me. My last season was so very short due to my illness, and I am quite anxious about Mama's expectations. Mama seems consumed with knowing all the London gossip. I feel certain she is up to something already. I would not be surprised if she has already selected matches for the both of us." Caroline paused, resting her hands at her side. She glanced up at Lucy seriously. "I cannot stomach the idea of marrying yet."

Lucy shook her head solemnly. "Caroline, you must not worry. Isn't it you that has always said you only listen to Mama when it suits you?"

Caroline felt her shoulders relax. She smiled. She did like upsetting her mother, but only in small matters. Lady Hopkins gave such good reactions. But this felt different, somehow. Caroline felt certain her mother was much more serious this time. "You are quite right, Lucy. I will make it my duty to follow my own advice. I may marry, but she won't have all the say. I will make it my concern to rally in support of my own happiness."

Lucy gripped Caroline's hand tightly. "Indeed! You must make it your concern to support my happiness as well, as I lack the strength to stand against Mama." Lucy's voice turned softer with a hint of sarcasm. "Please do not let me marry a grandpapa."

The girls laughed as they made their way back into the house. Lucy passed the trunks in the great hall and pulled Caroline's arm. "Tell me what dresses Louisa has packed for you. Did you bring your new pink linen gown? It would be lovely for the concerts."

Lucy appeared determined to make Caroline enjoy herself, and Lucy began detailing the outfits her sister would wear, including dresses of her own.

"We must purchase some new gowns. For in your gain, I also gain since we are nearly the same size. Until then, you may borrow any dress I bring," Lucy offered.

It was a kind gesture, and Caroline affectionately rested her head on Lucy's shoulder, but before Caroline could thank Lucy vocally, Louisa marched into the room with an unmistakably irritated expression spread across her face.

"Miss Lucy, Miss Caroline, you have visitors. Mr. Jasper and his mother have called upon you both. They are in the drawing room as we speak." Louisa held the door open in a gesture of command.

With mutual disgust, Caroline and Lucy made a collective sigh. They found their way to the drawing room all too quickly and found the son and mother standing impatiently. The Jaspers, the nearest neighbors to Whitefield Hall, felt it their duty to demoralize all they came in contact with, and, even worse, they felt it their duty as neighbors to call upon the young sisters almost weekly. The son, Charles, had always shown a liking for Lucy, a fact that Lucy seemed completely oblivious to. As always, Lucy was the perfect picture of hospitality and grace. Caroline found herself mechanically following Lucy's lead as she curtsied kindly to the pair of them and offered felicitous greetings.

"Mrs. Jasper, Mr. Jasper, how kind of you to call! How do you do?" Lucy said, offering her hand to Charles who took it only too eagerly. Caroline met Mrs. Jasper's smile with the same outward courtesy, albeit with inward contempt.

Mrs. Jasper, as per usual, seated herself on the finest chair, and was scanning the room in an arrogant manner. "We couldn't very well not call now could we, seeing how you are at present preparing to journey to London, and without a word or letter to me? I'd have thought your mother aware of such details. Your absence is, without exception, the most horrid news. Why, flying off to London in search of a husband? I know what you are thinking, and I will have none of it. It will not do to contradict me. I cannot understand the meaning of it all. There are so many young gentlemen here, in Chelmsford, that might satisfy the both of you and your mother."

The room became silent, both girls unsure of how to respond to the blunt woman. Caroline giggled uncomfortably, covering her mouth when Lucy nudged her.

"You have always been everything thoughtful, Ma'am," Caroline offered curtly, glancing sideways at Lucy.

Yes, Mrs. Jasper had always been everything thoughtful. Indeed, she had been thinking of nothing other than marrying her son Charles off to one of the Hopkins sisters for years. It would have been a compliment had Charles Jasper been anything other than the unpleasant man he was. His fixed smile seemed rigid, and he often drooled and spit as he spoke. His hair was already thinning, and the remaining wisps rested greasily against his elongated forehead. It was only to his detriment that his choice of attire and expression seemed to compliment his personality perfectly.

"Yes, Miss Lucy, we shall miss your company sorely. I myself might take the chance to go to London this season," Charles admitted, his gaze fixed on Lucy.

"Are you quite sure, Mr. Jasper?" Lucy asked. "You have not gone to London these past two seasons."

"I have some business in town I must attend to and have sent word for our townhome to be prepared for an extended stay. I feel much inclined to crumble to the temptations of town this year," Charles said, chuckling while saliva drooped around his mouth as he rallied his arm in the air enthusiastically.

Mrs. Jasper rolled her eyes dramatically and gave an annoyed sigh. "Oh, Charles. Do not talk so. Town holds little temptation for one such as you," she replied. She turned toward Lucy. "I cannot seem to understand why he must leave me. I am beginning to feel determined to accompany him."

Charles stood up straight and pushed his shoulders back even farther than usual. "Mother, you needn't accompany me. I am nearly thirty. I am quite capable of completing my business on my own."

"Perhaps you are, and perhaps you are not. I only say that I shall not have my only son leave me for months at a time. I am not quite the young woman I used to be. Without your father, I feel the loss of your presence keenly." Mrs. Jasper turned from her son abruptly, dropping her head into her hands.

Caroline cleared her throat. "Mrs. Jasper, how does your niece Miss Lenore do? I've heard she has become quite the accomplished painter."

Attempts at comforting Mrs. Jasper almost always went unnoticed, as Mrs. Jasper saw everyone and nearly everything below her. And yet, the mention of her niece was always sure to raise her spirit.

"I'd say! She could paint the king. It's quite a shame, but she has ruined my taste in art. I cannot stand the mediocre paintings I see that so often cover every wall of every home. I must have Georgiana stay, and then you will see my meaning. But, you might meet her in London. I shall write to her and have her stay in town with Charles and me."

"Certainly, Mrs. Jasper. It would be our pleasure," Lucy answered charmingly.

Caroline's eyes widened. She was sure nothing could convince her to visit the Jaspers while in town. Lucy glared at Caroline in warning, and Caroline's eyes lowered as she bit the side of her cheek to keep from grinning.

"And not only does she paint magnificently, but she is quite the beauty! She will be the talk of London this year, I tell you!" Mrs. Jasper sat up straighter as she spoke, forgetting her previous offended state. Her niece was her pride. Mrs. Jasper had wanted a daughter to dress up and parade around London more than anything, but all she had had was Charles. The poor niece suffered the shattered dreams of the aunt.

"And shall you enjoy London, Miss Lucy?" Charles turned toward Lucy as he spoke.

"Oh, yes! I have always enjoyed the entertainment and fashions. The company is always so agreeable as well."

"Hmphff. I had not thought you the London type," Charles said, pacing the whole of the room, sweat permeating his enormous forehead.

Caroline absentmindedly began tapping her foot in impatience. Lucy nudged her sister subtly once more in response and turned the conversation to the immediate demands that needed attending to before embarking on their travels. The Jaspers protested, Mrs. Jasper criticizing the efficiency of the estate if the daughters were to attend to such trivial matters.

However much duty they thought was owed to them as the nearest neighbor, Caroline was tempted to put them in their place. She could not stand such forced conversation or such impolite ramblings. Perhaps London would not be so dreadfully bad as Caroline had imagined. By the time Mrs. Jasper left with Charles, Caroline was positively glowing at the thought of departing Whitefield Hall.

For though the city offered no escape to Whitefield Hall, Whitefield Hall offered no escape from the Jaspers.

Chapter 4

The journey to London was nothing short of fatiguing for Caroline, though not in the physical sense. Between the three women, all conversation of town and the excitement for the season had been completely exhausted. Lady Hopkins had spouted off her usual lectures on gentility and manners at least two times to each of the girls. The journey had also allowed for short naps, all of which reminded Caroline just how loudly her mother snored.

After arriving in London, the three women spent the majority of the next day recovering. Caroline had felt fully recovered almost upon arrival, being hardly the type of lady to require much more than a walk or ride to restore her well-being. However, her mother and Lucy required time for improvement. Between warm baths, sleeping all day, and eating much more than was necessary, the two women's spirits were finally starting to be restored.

It was on the third morning since arriving to London that Caroline became especially restless. The house in London was so much smaller than Whitefield Hall, and its proximity to the neighbors left Caroline feeling trapped. She craved a moment away from the confining walls.

Caroline sat at the breakfast table, her plate undisturbed, as she eyed Lucy impatiently. Lucy, seemingly unaware of Caroline, only nibbled at her food, every so often glancing to Lord Hopkins as he read the newspaper, grunting or puffing sporadically. Caroline laid her fingers across the table, hoping to gently coax Lucy's attention away from her father.

"How are you feeling?" she asked. Lucy's face brightened. Caroline continued. "Shall we go out for the day? I long to leave this house."

The hint of a smile flashed across Lucy's face. She pressed her lips together as she eyed Caroline curiously. "I fear I am not wholly recovered from the journey."

Caroline shrugged, irritated by Lucy's words.

Lucy let out an amused giggle. "Oh, Caroline! I should have known better than to tease you. I think a walk by the shops is just the exercise I need. Shall we ask Mama if George may drive us to town? You are in such need of new gowns."

Caroline nodded. She was beginning to think that dress shopping would be preferable to sitting in the house all day.

Lucy tilted her head knowingly as she explained, "Why, just last week, I overheard Mama discussing our allowances with Papa. It is quite the sum this year. We are to attend the concert tomorrow evening. Perhaps we will find some ribbons to compliment your pink gown?"

Caroline nodded in support of the idea, while Lucy gave an excited squeal.

Lord Hopkins's eyes rose above the paper suspiciously, only offering muted chuckles and a mumbled, "What excitement a girl finds in the latest fashions, I shall never attempt to discover."

Caroline watched as Lucy eagerly stepped into Mrs. Privett's dress shop. A young woman with dark hair and a bright smile stood at the entrance to greet them. She curtsied gracefully and offered her services. Caroline stood cautiously at the door, watching curiously as Lucy began telling the young saleswoman of their pressing needs.

Caroline roamed the dressing counters, pausing every so often to inspect a fabric or notion more closely. She did not detest shopping by any means, but Caroline found herself at a loss in choosing one item from another. Lucy, however timid in other areas, did not have the least hesitation when it came to such decisions, and she took no thought but to take responsibility for Caroline's needs.

Before Caroline knew it, Lucy had ordered at least four gowns for Caroline, insisting Caroline could not do without even one of them. Caroline had nodded in amusement to the dressmaker, only daring to offer a fabric suggestion for the ball gown. Lucy had then spent another hour purchasing coordinating ribbons, bonnets, and gloves for each new dress ordered. Caroline admired the emerald silk Lucy had agreed upon for the ball gown. It was to be trimmed in ivory lace and would have the most delicate ruffles in the back. Lucy had also found a pretty, yet simple, white muslin frock, a gold and white afternoon dress, and a terracotta evening gown with beautiful embroidered white flowers in the sleeves and hem.

The girls left the dress shop arm in arm. The Hopkins sisters received more than a few admiring glances as they walked along the cobblestones, stopping to look at a shop window every so often along the way. At last they found themselves staring up at a sign hanging from an awning. It read, "Clark's Custom Cordwainer."

Lucy beamed. "This is the newest shop along Bishop Street. It opened just six months ago, and it is the talk of all London. Mr. Thomas Clark is a famous shoemaker; he recently returned from Paris after apprenticing one of Paris's finest cordwainers. I heard Mr. Clark recently completed a pair of boots for the Duke of Rembridge!"

Caroline scanned the front of the shop. The brick exterior had been freshly mortared, the door recently painted black, and the windows elegantly draped in red velvet curtains. In one window appeared a magnificent pair of men's riding boots with extravagant detailing on the leather. A small card next to the boots read, "Crafted for Lord Searly, Duke and Earl of Rembridge."

"I am astonished, Lucy," Caroline said mockingly, "that you would even consider such a shop. We are far beneath the notice of dukes and duchesses for our father is only a baron."

Lucy grinned. She slicked a strand of hair back as she attempted to imitate her mother. "Oh, come now, Caroline. You must know that we shall mingle with the very finest of crowds here. You must look your part." She paused, looking at the boots in the window once more. "Mama was here just yesterday requesting that our names be added to the list of Mr. Clark's clients," Lucy explained, reaching for the door.

The interior of the shop was small, though clean and orderly. A few shoes with cards were displayed on a shelf. A couple of clean sketches were framed upon the wall, and a curtain hung neatly behind the clerk's desk.

"Ladies, how may I be of service?" A young bookish gentleman asked as he stretched out his arms. His red hair was fixed to the latest fashion, with a single curl that cascaded down the left side of his forehead.

"Good day," Lucy said with a smile, "Miss Lucy Hopkins and Miss Caroline Hopkins here for measurements."

The clerk glanced at the appointment book on the desk, running his finger down a list, until at last he paused, and said softly, "Ah, you have come at just the right time. We seem to have an opening before our next customer. Please, follow me."

The clerk led the women to a booth behind the curtain. He gestured to an upholstered bench. "If you will please be seated, I will notify Mr. Clark you are here." The clerk then swung in a swift and graceful motion past the booth, humming softly.

Caroline and Lucy began chatting about the morning's excitement, when a man with broad shoulders entered the room. He was much younger than Caroline had imagined, appearing to be no older than thirty, and he wore a dark suit underneath a white apron. His black curly hair hung around his face and framed his dark eyes.

The clerk gestured toward the sisters. "And here they are, sir. Miss Lucy Hopkins and her sister Miss Caroline Hopkins."

The man nodded, hardly glancing to their faces. "And how may I be of service to you ladies?"

Lucy glanced at Caroline, her eyes brightening. "My sister and I are both in need of new boots and ballroom slippers. An elegant black boot would do nicely for each of us, but we have not yet decided on the details of the slippers."

Mr. Clark nodded. "Allow me a moment to measure. It will take time for me to carve the last. Perhaps by then you will have considered the details?" He turned toward his clerk, offering a mumbled command. The clerk nodded and whispered in return. Mr. Clark reached into his apron pocket, pulling out a few measuring tools. "The molds should be done within the week. Would you like a note sent to your address when they are finished? We can schedule an appointment to discuss the design then."

Lucy smiled. "Yes. We shall leave it with your clerk."

Mr. Clark nodded but did not smile. Caroline wondered if she had ever seen such a serious man. Mr. Clark knelt in front of Lucy and carefully removed her boot. Caroline found she could not look away from his face. His dark eyelashes were thick and blocked her view of his eyes. His jaw was square and strong, like the rest of him. She watched as he concentrated, measuring Lucy's foot in multiple places and repeating the numbers aloud to the clerk. When Mr. Clark reached Caroline, she felt her whole face blush, but he did not even look up to see it.

"As I said before, I will send word when your molds are completed. An appointment to discuss leathers, fabrics, embellishments and the like will follow." He turned toward the clerk to give some direction before rising to his feet and offering his hand to Lucy and Caroline as they stood from the bench.

Caroline held his gaze, still curious of Mr. Clark's seemingly pronounced seriousness.

The shop bell rang.

Caroline was still staring, when she found herself impulsively addressing Mr. Clark. "And will you display my boots the same as you did Lord Searly's riding boots?" she teased. "I suppose that luxury is only reserved for your most *prestigious* clients."

Mr. Clark was taken by surprise, but before he could answer, Caroline heard a deep laugh as a tall gentleman entered the small booth and replied, "Perhaps he shall put yours on a pedestal above mine."

Caroline blushed. She looked to the ground and offered a small curtsy to the gentleman she could only assume was the famous duke.

"Your Grace, I trust you received my note that your boots had been completed?" Mr. Clark inquired.

With Lord Searly's attention on Mr. Clark, Caroline dared to look upon the duke amidst her embarrassment. The man was just what one might expect a young duke to be. He was indeed handsome with honey colored eyes and a clear complexion. His brown hair was styled effortlessly, and he was dressed in an extremely elegant fashion. The duke also seemed to possess a certain commanding presence that was impossible to ignore. He looked to be in his late twenties.

"Yes, yes. I believe the whole town has been admiring the boots these past days. Splendid! You are quite the craftsman, Mr. Clark. May I inquire as to the names of the young ladies here at present?" He turned toward Caroline and Lucy.

"Miss Lucy Hopkins and her sister Miss Caroline Hopkins," the clerk offered.

Lord Searly offered a low bow.

"How do you do, Your Grace?" Caroline asked without meeting his gaze.

He laughed, clearly amused at Caroline's embarrassment. "Much better now that I know your name. And have you been in London long?"

"We have only just arrived," Lucy explained calmly.

"Yes, I see. Ordering dresses, shoes, and the like . . . how ever shall London keep up with you?" Lord Searly chuckled to himself once more. "And shall you be attending any concerts this week? There is no better entertainment to be had in London save a ball."

Caroline sensed the man was being sarcastic, but forced herself to answer politely. "We are to attend a concert at Lee Hall tomorrow evening, my lord."

Lord Searly nodded, smiling much too openly at Caroline.

She tried to collect herself, shaking softly as she turned to Mr. Clark. "We shall await your note for our appointment, Mr. Clark. Good day, Your Grace," Caroline offered as she curtsied and brushed past the gentlemen.

Lucy followed, offering her farewell. Mr. Clark only nodded.

"Good day, Miss Lucy, Miss Caroline. I hope we shall meet again soon," Lord Searly offered with a smug look upon his face.

The girls were silent as they entered the carriage. Caroline had never been more mortified in her life! To meet Lord Searly under such conditions, especially as she had been mocking his displayed boots! She felt completely ridiculous.

To add to her humiliation, Lucy was struggling to hold back from laughing. "Lord Searly was most agreeable, was he not, Caroline?" Lucy asked.

Caroline rolled her eyes at the mention of their meeting. "I suppose he was, for a duke. Did you not think he thought me quite ridiculous?"

Lucy giggled. "He was only teasing you. I'm sure he knew you were not serious. His boots have caused quite the stir, but how could they not? I've never seen such magnificent riding boots." Lucy's voice began to drift off as she looked out the carriage window, watching the people move up and down the street. "What a coincidental meeting. Mama will be so pleased."

Caroline fell silent, and remained so as the carriage stopped at the home of Miss Kensington, Lucy's dear friend from the previous season. It was a happy reunion, but Caroline still felt the effects of her humiliation, and in turn, was not an exciting conversant. Miss Kensington had stolen Lucy's hand and pulled her onto the sofa, divulging the recent gossip and news. Caroline stood unmoved by it all, and was only shaken to reality by Lucy's announcement that she and Caroline were expected home.

When they returned home, Lady Hopkins greeted the pair in the best of spirits. "Girls! Girls! You will never guess who has just sent us an invitation! Lord Searly—the most handsome and eligible bachelor of London!" Lady Hopkins took Caroline by a shoulder with one hand, while grasping Lucy's arm with the other. "He has invited us to his ball in two weeks. I confess I am shocked, but what a compliment! I do believe we shall run with the top this year."

Joseph ran his eyes across the cordwainer shop book, stopping at a small scribbled name. "I see you have scheduled an appointment for Miss Lucy and Miss Caroline next week. Shall I send them a note?"

Thomas nodded, his attention clearly fixed to the wood in front of him.

Joseph smiled. "The sisters were quite pretty, were they not? May I ask which of the sisters you prefer?"

Thomas began carving more intensely, refusing to make a reply.

Joseph continued to pry, gesturing as he explained, "I would not have thought twice of them, had it not been the way the younger one addressed you. If I had not known better, I would have sworn she was attempting to flirt with you."

The right corner of Thomas's lips twitched as he attempted to suppress a smile. "And if I had not known better, Joseph, I would think you were neglecting your post at the front of the store."

Joseph moved nervously, laughing only when he was a safe distance away from Thomas.

Chapter 5

The concert was greatly attended. As hard as she tried, Lady Hopkins could not settle her nerves. Lucy looked charming, as usual, while Caroline possessed an even more striking appearance than customary. More than a few gentlemen of significant worth had already introduced themselves to Lord and Lady Hopkins. The evening seemed to be the perfect reintroduction into society for the girls.

However, it was during the second set of songs that a small commotion arose as Lord Jonathon Searly entered the hall. Each mother seemed to be eyeing the duke as the quintessential matrimonial prize for her respective daughter. The duke passed the rows of onlookers silently, only gesturing to wave several times to gentlemen acquaintances, and made his way to an empty seat near the Hopkins Family. Following Lord Searly was a younger gentleman.

Lady Hopkins could not help but notice the duke sneak a few admiring glances at Caroline, though Caroline seemed oblivious to the attention. The duke was just the sort of man Lady Hopkins hoped Caroline would attract! Certainly they would meet at the ball next week.

The second set of music came to an end. The audience stood and applauded the musicians, prompting a short but beautiful encore. And at last the musicians took their place in the mingling crowd, exchanging words with the attentive audience. Lady Hopkins had resumed scanning the room when she felt a soft tap on her shoulder. A young gentleman was respectfully bowing. Lady Hopkins recognized the duke peering up at her face.

"Lady Hopkins, what a delight. I remember meeting you some time ago. However then, I did not think you old enough to have two grown daughters of your own." Lord Searly gestured to Lucy and Caroline.

Lady Hopkins smiled, color rising to her cheeks as she curtsied. "Your Grace, it has been some time. You remember my husband, Lord Phillip Hopkins?"

Lord Searly bowed. "Hopkins, it is good to see you again."

Lord Hopkins bowed his head ever so gently, and replied sarcastically, "And you, Lord Searly. May I inquire as to why I am honored with your attention?"

The duke began to laugh, while Lady Hopkins placed a reprimanding hand on her husband's arm. "I did not know you enjoyed concerts at Lee Hall, my lord," she said, hoping to prolong the conversation.

"I confess I have not attended Lee's for these past two years, but I have been informed that this year's musicians are much improved, as is the company at present," Lord Searly declared. "Come, you must introduce me to your two daughters."

"You are quite right, Your Grace," said Lady Hopkins. "I present to you my eldest, Lucy, and my second daughter, Caroline."

Lord Searly smiled. "Your daughters do you credit, Lady Hopkins. And I can assure you, the pleasure is all mine. I do not recall ever seeing such pleasant faces."

Caroline's cheeks rose to a blush, and Lady Hopkins was surprised to see her daughter's stern expression. Lord Searly quietly chuckled and winked at Caroline, seemingly unaware of Lady Hopkins's watchful eye.

"Lady Hopkins, may I present my cousin, Mr. Frandsen?"

The young man beside Lord Searly bowed graciously and took Lady Hopkins's hand. He had a genuine look about him. Although fashionable and tidy, he did not appear pretentious. He was not as tall as the duke. He stood just a mere six inches above Lucy and lacked the physique of his famous cousin. His dusty blond hair and dark eyes were pleasant but far from handsome.

"Have you been in London long, Mr. Frandsen?" Lucy asked.

"I'm afraid I've been here much too long. I've been in town for nearly four years, excepting a few short summer stays at Lord Searly's estate."

Lord Searly took a step closer to Caroline. Lady Hopkins could not help but smile approvingly.

"I do not recall meeting you these last two seasons," remarked Lucy.

"I have not been up to the task of socializing. I admit I often prefer my books and study to a party of people I have not met," Mr. Frandsen replied, pausing as if he sensed his social ineptness. "That is—I suppose I am more practiced in studying than I am in conversing."

Lucy's hand rose quickly to her mouth to hide the giggle that had already escaped.

"And what do you study, Mr. Frandsen?" Lady Hopkins asked, leaning toward him.

"All sorts. I particularly enjoy the sciences, but I find the occasional book on economics to my liking as well. Unlike my cousin here, I shall have to take up employment, and I have made it my duty to discover what would suit me best."

"And have you discovered it?" Lucy asked, a shy tone in her voice.

"Yes, I suppose I have. Lord Searly demands I manage his country estate. In any case, I cannot refuse, seeing how I spent many summers there and think of it as home."

"How generous of your cousin," remarked Lord Hopkins.

"Anything but generous, sir," added Lord Searly, shaking his head. "For I shall enjoy his presence and watching him labor in my behalf!"

Lord Hopkins began to laugh, though Lady Hopkins doubted it was for the same reason the duke laughed. She recognized her husband's mocking tone.

"Lady Hopkins, Lord Hopkins, ladies, forgive me. I must catch an old acquaintance before they leave. I hope I may see you at my ball in two weeks?" the duke asked.

Lady Hopkins curtsied. "Depend upon it, my lord."

Lord Searly climbed into his carriage in the best of spirits. He had seen all of the pretty ladies in London for nearly six seasons, but he had seldom come across as charming of a girl as Miss Caroline

Hopkins. Her beauty was inherent, but it was her manner that intrigued him most. Although young and inexperienced, he sensed her spirit. He felt most determined to become acquainted with her. And while he also noticed her attempts to ignore his attention, he was sure she felt it.

"Jonathon, you spoke to merely five people at the assembly hall. What are you scheming?" Mr. Frandsen asked bluntly.

The carriage began to sway along the stone street. Lord Searly could not conceal his amusement as he smiled mischievously. "David, you must not worry. I am simply trying to have some entertainment this season, and I have discovered it in Miss Caroline Hopkins!"

Mr. Frandsen fidgeted with his coat as he appeared to consider his cousin's words. At last, Mr. Frandsen shook his head disapprovingly. "You cannot be serious? The girl comes from a fine family. I do not think Lord Hopkins would allow anything improper to pass his notice."

Lord Searly broke out in laughter. "David, my boy, I do not plan on anything as dreadful as what you suppose. I only mean to toy with the girl. You must allow me a kiss or two from her if I am inconspicuous enough."

"You—subtle in any sort of manner?" Mr. Frandsen looked to Lord Searly in disbelief.

"Don't look so concerned! I might rise to the occasion. Have you ever seen such lovely eyes?"

David fell silent for a moment. "No, I don't think I have seen lovelier eyes in all of London."

Lord Searly grinned; he was certain it was not Miss Caroline's eyes that had captured his cousin's attention so completely.

CHAPTER 6

It was five days after the concert, and Lady Hopkins could still talk of nothing else but Lord Searly. Lord Searly this, and Lord Searly that! Couldn't Caroline just die, he was so handsome? Wasn't it just too much that the duke had singled out Lady Hopkins and her daughters?

Caroline tried to distract herself, but her mother had seen the duke's particular interest in Caroline, and Lady Hopkins took every possible moment to instruct Caroline of her duty to her family to encourage him. Caroline felt certain that was one thing she need *not* do, for out of all the men of the ton, Lord Searly seemed to be the man *least* in need of encouragement!

The truth was that Caroline did not like to draw attention to herself. She did not care to have any more eyes drawn to her than what already were. Lord Searly, on the other hand, was just the type of man that seemed to enjoy such attention. In fact, his presence demanded it. All the lips of London could scarcely speak of anything else. His name was quite unavoidable.

Caroline allowed herself only once to ponder the man's elegant features—his tall frame, brown hair, and honey-colored eyes. She felt her heart beat fast just thinking of him. He was handsome, but so much so that the man knew it and did not seem better because of it.

Lucy had been far too busy to notice Caroline's blush at the mere mention of the duke. It was not that Lucy was neglectful, but rather Lucy seemed to be in a fever herself, a fever of confusion. Lucy had had three visits from gentlemen in the last five days. Mr. Jenkins, from the previous seasons, upon renewing his acquaintance with her at the concert, had taken the liberty to call on Lucy. He had been polite and engaging, but Caroline groaned when she thought of his glossy eyes and the way they never left Lucy for the full twenty minutes, even alongside Lady Hopkins. Caroline had sat in a nearby chair, pretending to be consumed by her embroidery. But to sit before a lady and her mother and show such puppy-faced indulgence was more than degrading. How Mr. Jenkins had endured it, Caroline was not sure. Lucy had looked relieved at Mr. Jenkins's departure, but she did not mention it other than to answer Lady Hopkins's inquiries about his hat and coat and the state of his dreadful coach.

Then there was Charles Jasper. The poor fellow had indeed come to London in an effort to protect his prime objective. He would not allow another man to rob him of Lucy. Charles's attention to Lucy was as always, quite disturbing. Caroline had counted how many times he had spit as he spoke. The count was nearly twenty. Caroline also could not help but notice the poor condition of his thinning hair. He had actually attempted to style it much like Lord Searly's—curls mounted in a mop on top of his head. Sadly, Charles's hair was much more reminiscent of a ratted hair ball slicked in grease.

It was clear that Charles had indulged himself more often since arriving in London, for his belly now hung quite awkwardly over his thin frame. Caroline had endured his talk of his cousin, the lovely and exceptional Miss Georgiana Lenore, and it was not until he had extended the invitation for Lucy and Caroline to call upon Miss Lenore that Caroline became irritable. Caroline had tried to object, but Lady Hopkins had insisted the girls would visit in the coming weeks; for it was only fitting they exhibit the kindness expected of such close neighbors.

Lucy's third suitor was, however, quite unexpected. Mr. Frandsen, Lord Searly's young cousin, had sent a letter to Lady Hopkins two days prior asking permission to call on the family. Lady Hopkins, anticipating a certain cousin that would accompany Mr. Frandsen, sent word straight away to him that he was most welcome. A friend of the duke, or better yet, cousin of Lord Searly, was always welcome in Lady Hopkins's home, especially if it was to see one or both of her daughters.

Mr. Frandsen arrived exactly at eleven o'clock. He arrived in a burgundy coat and brown trousers. His hair was neatly styled, and he carried a book at his side. Bentley had directed him to the east drawing room where the three women were waiting.

Lady Hopkins's disappointment upon discovering him unaccompanied was much too obvious. Caroline shook her head in embarrassment.

"Lady Hopkins," Mr. Frandsen said as he took her hand. He did not hesitate to turn toward Lucy. He bowed. "Miss Lucy and Miss Caroline, it is a pleasure to see you both looking so well. How do you do?"

Lucy had almost made her reply, when Lady Hopkins mistook his inquiry to be about herself. "Oh, we are most comfortably settled, I assure you, though it has only been a week since our arrival. Our estate is just north of Chelmsford in Essex. You must know the place." Lady Hopkins looked up at Mr. Frandsen and noticed he was flushed. She cleared her throat. "How silly of me! I did not even offer you a seat. Please, be seated, Mr. Frandsen. How do you do? And your cousin, Lord Searly?"

There was no mistaking the way in which she said *Lord Searly.* Caroline recognized her mother's impatient tone. It was apparent that Mr. Frandsen also caught Lady Hopkins's emphasis, for his brow furrowed and he swallowed uncomfortably. "I am well. Lord Searly sends his regards. He is looking forward to seeing each of you at his ball next week. He has had little time to attend to all the details. The guest list and arrangements are not yet settled. I hope you will forgive him for his absence this morning."

This seemed to satisfy Lady Hopkins, and after a few minutes, she kindly excused herself. Mr. Frandsen nodded in acknowledgement as Lady Hopkins left the room.

The girls sat in silence for a few minutes as a housemaid brought in a tray of tea and crackers.

"You must have a cup of tea," Lucy sweetly offered. She poured Mr. Frandsen a cup, extending it toward him.

"And what book do you carry with you, sir?" Caroline inquired.

The rattling of the cup against the saucer signaled his surprise, as he handed the small book to Caroline. "It is an old book I have been studying. It is not my usual course of study, but I do find it has fully engaged my interest."

Caroline glanced at the worn cover. *The Nature of Condition.*

"What is it about?" Caroline asked, genuinely interested.

"It is a discourse on the station of one's birth and the consequences of the said condition." Mr. Frandsen smiled and paused. "It is very philosophical, much too boring and, perhaps, too forward-thinking for such a meeting as this."

Caroline smiled at his modesty, stifling a giggle as she watched Lucy gaze at the man in open admiration. Lucy had absentmindedly filled her cup to the brim, a small trickle running down its side. Mr. Frandsen did not seem to notice Lucy as she quietly wiped her cup.

But Caroline struggled to ignore Lucy's mishap. She cleared her throat, determined to prevent her sister from embarrassment. "Oh, but I am intrigued. And how does one overcome one's station? By simple ambition?" She sipped her tea, patiently awaiting his response.

"It is not as easy or as simple as that. It is not a book about ambition, but rather a discourse on men, and the divergent ways in which one may learn to overcome society's expectations of oneself."

"Quite the forward-thinking book, wouldn't you agree, Lucy? And what would your cousin say to such thinking? Surely he does not plan to put off society's expectations of him?" asked Caroline with a twinkle in her eye.

Mr. Frandsen began to laugh. "I assure you my cousin would call such a book rubbish. My cousin sometimes complains of all that is expected of him, but I'm sure he celebrates his great luck in being born to such a station. Would not all men?" Mr. Frandsen glanced more intently at Lucy.

Caroline did not think there was a single thing that Lord Searly concealed. He seemed abominably proud of his situation in life. Only a true friend, or biased relation, could have such an optimistic estimation of the duke's character.

"I am sure he will make his family proud, Mr. Frandsen." Lucy smiled. "As will you. When will you begin managing his estate? And have you no estate of your own?"

The sound of Mr. Frandsen's cup against the saucer again signaled his surprise. He apologetically smiled and straightened his coat. "I possess a small country home, which I inherited from my father. It is not large, but it is quite beautifully situated. I shall take over management of the country estate next year."

"I think we shall be wonderful friends, Mr. Frandsen," exclaimed Caroline. "I am not sure I have met a gentleman quite so grounded. Anyone associated with you might count themselves lucky."

Mr. Frandsen blushed. "I am flattered, Miss Caroline, but were you to know many of the men that our society deems below our rank, you would find there are a great many grounded gentlemen right here in London."

Caroline smiled at that. "Perhaps you are right. I hope I shall meet many more, though I do not have expectations of a great many with half the qualities you possess, Mr. Frandsen."

Mr. Frandsen fidgeted with the book in his hands, tapping his thumb across its title. "You must come to know my cousin, Lord Searly, then. Jonathon, though he is frivolous when it comes to the luxuries he is so entitled to, has many admirable attributes."

"Indeed?" Caroline's eyebrows rose as she studied Mr. Frandsen's expression. She wondered if he had been sent to put in a good word for the duke.

Mr. Frandsen only nodded and rose to his feet. "Ladies, I do apologize, but I have lost track of time. I am late for another appointment. I hope you will forgive me. It has been a most enjoyable visit. I hope to see you at the ball?" His eyes met Lucy's face.

"Why of course, sir." Lucy said sweetly. She rose to her feet.

"Then may I have the pleasure of your company for the first two dances, Miss Lucy?"

Lucy's cheeks colored, but her composure did not weaken. "It would be my pleasure, Mr. Frandsen."

Caroline attempted to conceal her amused smile. Mr. Frandsen's desire to call was quite of its own accord. Caroline's opinion of Lord Searly's cousin had, within just one sitting, risen far above her opinion of the duke.

It was two days later that Mr. Clark's note of appointment arrived. Lady Hopkins accompanied Caroline and Lucy as they made their way down the bustling London streets to the shop. The same red-haired clerk greeted them and offered them seats in a separate room furnished with a small drafting table and cushioned seating. The women waited in silence for Mr. Clark.

Caroline studied the small room. The table had several designs laid out and beside them were a few samples of fabrics and beads. The walls were covered with a gold patterned paper, complementing the large framed mirror that hung above the table. If it had not been for the strong smell of wood, leather, and polishes, Caroline might have forgotten she was in a shop and not a small sitting room. Though it was not extravagant, the shop was kept fashionable and tidy.

Caroline's thoughts were interrupted by the sound of footsteps.

"Good morning, ladies," Mr. Clark said as he offered a small bow. His smile seemed polite, if not a bit rigid.

As the women greeted Mr. Clark and offered their how-do-you-dos, Mr. Clark placed two sets of carved lasts on the table. Caroline picked one up, inspecting it carefully. The wooden molds were meticulously carved in the pattern of her own foot.

"I have finished your lasts, and have endeavored to begin sewing the boots and slipper liners. I need only to discuss the details of design before they are completed," Mr. Clark began.

Caroline could not help but gaze into his handsome face. A small dimple between his chin and cheek appeared whenever he spoke, and the result was simply charming. His every move spoke of confidence and independence, yet Caroline could not gather any clue as to the man himself.

Lady Hopkins clapped her hands together. "I am not astonished one whit, Mr. Clark. I would not wish for any other cordwainer in all of England or beyond." Lady Hopkins seemed to have meant it as a compliment, but the tone was condescending.

Mr. Clark paid no heed, however, and began inquiring about fabrics and embellishments.

As Lucy and Caroline sorted through the piles of sketches, Lady Hopkins continued to instruct Mr. Clark. "Now the ball gown slippers must be elegant but simple. Although I dote on my daughters exceedingly, I would not wish a gentleman to find them too frivolous."

"I see, Lady Hopkins." Mr. Clark replied. "Shall I endeavor to make the slippers elegant yet ordinary?" His brows were furrowed in what Caroline could only guess was quiet amusement.

Lady Hopkins laughed. "Just so, sir! You must indulge me! I wish you to design the slippers as you see fit. Perhaps the boots as well, for I see you are ahead of me. Please, Caroline, Lucy, come stand before Mr. Clark. He shall look at you and see the style I have so poorly attempted to describe. Perhaps you would design them better yourself now that you know the fabric color, Mr. Clark?"

Mr. Clark stared at the lasts for a moment, placing his hands on his hips. "I would not wish to disappoint, Lady Hopkins. I have never designed shoes without input from my customers. You must have some requests. Perhaps you can choose one of these designs," he offered, gesturing to some sketches lying on the table.

Lady Hopkins waved her hand at him in refusal. "As I have just explained, I think we shall be better off leaving it to you! Now, do observe my daughters. Do you not see their seemingly effortless elegance?"

Mr. Clark looked toward Lucy. Lucy stood straight but did not meet his gaze. Mr. Clark nodded, as if to say he had captured her style. He then studied Caroline. Caroline could feel him assessing her. And though she knew his intent, she felt he was instead studying her character. At last she met his gaze. His dark eyes scanned her face, causing Caroline to blush.

Mr. Clark nodded and turned away. "I shall endeavor to please you, Lady Hopkins."

Lady Hopkins stood, smiling at her daughters. "We look forward to the finished product, Mr. Clark." She paused, slowly raising a finger to her chin. "Is there no possibility of the slippers being completed by this week? We are to attend Lord Searly's ball this Friday."

Mr. Clark only sighed. "I will finish the slippers straight away, Lady Hopkins." He gave a slight bow.

The women curtsied and took their leave.

Caroline could not help but look back at Mr. Clark. He leaned against the table, his broad shoulders and arms gripping the edges, as if he studied the fabric patches before him, but Caroline noted he was instead watching her.

Thomas had not stirred from the table of swatches and notions for quite some time. His sketches were almost complete when Joseph interrupted his thoughts with a snide remark.

"I see you are still working on the sketches for Miss Caroline's slippers. Shall I order gold trimmings for the lady? I see you wish her slippers to be the finest." Joseph was smiling, leaning against the booth's frame.

Thomas cast a dark glance at him, and spouted off the first words that came to his mind. "By all means, if you like the lady so much. I am apt to subtract the cost from your pay!" He then threw the book of swatches across the room playfully, the impact sending Joseph sideways into a heap of crumpled sketches upon the floor. Thomas laughed as he scratched his head and released an unintentional sigh.

Chapter 7

Lord Hopkins studied the card next to the flowers.

To Miss Caroline Hopkins,
Please allow me the first two dances.
Your humble servant,
Jonathon Searly

Lord Hopkins flinched, dropping the card to the table. It did not feel like it had been long ago that he had been courting Miss Eleanor Davenport.

Uncle Whitison had all but ruined him, until Lord Hopkins had caught the eye of the charming Miss Eleanor Davenport. Everyone had called him lucky, and perhaps he was, but Lord Hopkins could not shake the guilt he had battled for years. He had loved Eleanor, almost from the start, but he had known of her fortune from the beginning.

Of course he had grown to love her deeply, but his heart had almost broken when Lady Hopkins had discovered his financial situation. And though he was not all she had wanted him to be, she had never been anything but mindful of him. Lady Hopkins was a dutiful wife. She was an even greater mother. Lord Hopkins could think of nothing more beautiful to him than the image of Lady Hopkins. He adored her, and he told her often by way of flirtatious compliments and looks. But his wife had not seemed to hear it. Or, at least, she did not believe him anymore.

Lord Hopkins stared at the card before him from Lord Searly. Lord Searly, Duke and Earl of Rembridge, who knew so little of life and so much of comfort and entitlement, was attempting to court his Caroline. Of course the duke's attention should have been an honor to him, but instead Lord Hopkins felt instinctively protective. What could Caroline gain from Lord Searly besides even more fortune? Lord Hopkins shuddered as he pictured his youngest daughter battling the guilt that had plagued him for so many years. No, Phillip had learned it was better to marry for love than for fortune. Yet, Lady Hopkins had her heart set upon the match now. He could not stand to think of offending his wife, not when he had already proved to be such a general disappointment to her. *No*, Phillip decided, he would not intervene. Caroline could always stand upon her own two feet. It freed Lord Hopkins's soul when he watched Caroline. She lived without regret, a trait he had once prided himself for.

Lucy and Caroline descended the stairs. Lord Hopkins watched in astonishment as they came to his side. "My girls have become women right before my eyes," he happily exclaimed. He grasped their hands, holding them at a distance to admire them. Finally, satisfied, he added, "There could not be two prettier little women in all the town!"

Lucy smiled, hesitating.

Caroline happily embraced her father, kissing him sweetly on the cheek. "Oh Papa! I shall never understand why you dote on us so."

This remark brought a smirk to Lord Hopkins's face. He shook his head in denial. "And I shall now have to play the part of the protective father, I see. For you both will have the lot after you!"

Lucy slipped her hand in his arm as she tenderly whispered, "Papa, I have missed you so. Shall you dance with me tonight?"

"But of course! You think I shall leave it all to the suitors? Not on my life!" He kissed Lucy on the cheek. As Caroline began to show her father her new green slippers that had been delivered earlier that morning, his attention turned to the stairs where Lady Hopkins now stood. Though she had matured over the years, her face was just as beautiful to him as it had been the night he had first kissed her.

"Lucy, on second thought, I do not know if I will be able to dance with you. I think I shall have to keep your mother beside me all evening. Some young suitor might try to snatch her up."

Lady Hopkins blushed but waved her hand in dismissal. Her eyes glistened in the darkly lit foyer. "I shall not mind what your father says, girls, for he is set on teasing me tonight."

Lord Hopkins left his daughters to take Lady Hopkins by the hand. "You shall not avoid my compliments so easily. I feel as if we are both twenty years younger and I am seeing you for the first time at old Ravenhurst's party."

"Girls, I am beginning to think your father has turned mad," Lady Hopkins said calmly, as she once more dismissed his compliment while directing everyone out the door. She stopped suddenly, inspecting Caroline's new gown.

"I cannot understand why you chose such a color, my dear. It's not the fashion at all." Lady Hopkins paused, looking Caroline up and down once more. A small smile spread across her powdered cheeks. "And yet, it suits you so well. There will not be another like it."

The ballroom was overcrowded and already overheating despite the efforts of Lord Searly's staff. Caroline found herself caught in a cloud of conversation and anxiety as she shuffled past the clusters of ladies perched along the edges of the room. Never had Caroline seen such a fantastic room. At nearly every opportune spot sat a magnificent flower arrangement. The colors were soft, muted tones, and seemed to accent nearly every detail of the room's furnishings. The aroma of the arrangements filled the entire room with a fresh and feminine scent that overpowered the already perspiring occupants. They were the same flowers that Lord Searly had sent to Caroline, the same flowers Louisa had placed in Caroline's extravagantly styled hair that evening.

Lord Searly greeted Caroline upon her arrival, as he had all of his guests. He had straight away commented on the blossoms in her dark hair and had not even attempted to disguise his pleasure. The duke swiftly took her hand and kissed it softly, his eyes lingering on her own. The effect of such a gesture left Caroline feeling even more heated than she already was.

The duke had then bent his head rather low toward her ear and whispered, "And shall I have the pleasure of your company for the first two dances?"

The words sent shivers down her back, and Caroline laughed nervously, offering a simple, "But of course, Your Grace."

From the corner of her eye, Caroline saw her mother watching their exchange. Caroline was mortified to see that her mother made no effort to hide her satisfaction, shifting her shoulders back proudly while sticking up her nose. Furthermore, the display had not gone unnoticed by the crowded corridor, and Caroline felt the eyes of many bearing down upon her. She curtsied elegantly to Lady Searly, the silver-haired duchess that remained a step or two behind her son, and Caroline quickly shuffled through the crowd in hopes of overcoming her embarrassment.

The musicians were tuning their instruments. Lady Hopkins was now seated near Caroline, clearly bored with the conversation of Mr. Jenkins. Though the man spoke to her mother, Caroline knew immediately that it was not her mother he longed to see. *Poor Lucy,* Caroline thought. *Thank goodness Charles Jasper is not here as well!*

The orchestra began to play an opening number, and Lord Searly approached Caroline, offering his arm. Caroline had not anticipated the attention that followed as the duke led her to the middle of the floor. The thought that she would lead the ball had never entered her distracted thoughts, and she was sorry for her thoughtless acceptance of such an offer.

Couples were now following the pair. Caroline's nerves were only made worse when she passed a mother and daughter standing near the circle.

"And who is she to lead the dance?" asked the mother in a disapproving tone. The daughter, no older than Caroline, pursed her lips and shook her head of curls in response. The mother continued. "It seems Lord Searly has forgotten his manners. He must have been distracted by that hideous dress."

Caroline straightened her shoulders, reminding herself to ignore the jealous looks and idle chatter. She glanced down at the emerald silk of her dress.

Lord Searly must have heard the gossip and sensed Caroline's nervousness. He smiled warmly. "I think your dress is quite beautiful, a nice change from the pinks and pastels. I find it most becoming."

The music was lovely, and Lord Searly danced gracefully. It was not long until Caroline forgot the staring bystanders, the silly gossip, and her own strained nerves. The twirls and enthusiasm of the other dancers only added to her enjoyment.

Lord Searly gave a small chuckle. "I am glad to see you are finally at ease, but are you always such a quiet and concentrated dancer?"

Caroline managed a small laugh. "I'm sorry, Your Grace. I am afraid I lost myself to the music and dancing. I have not seen such a ballroom."

"You like it then?"

"Of course, though I do not know the meaning of leading the ball with me. I have scarcely met you but two times."

"Can you not guess at my meaning?"

Caroline fell silent. She knew his bluntness should not irritate her, but his arrogant manners bothered her.

"And really, you must stop calling me Your Grace. It is entirely too formal, for we are to be friends. You shall call me Jonathon."

"Is that right? I am to call you Jonathon and we are to be friends?" She pulled back from his grip as she seriously responded, "I won't call you Jonathon. You are a duke. It is not proper."

"Then Lord Jonathon?" Lord Searly spun her elegantly, but when she returned to him, he brought her even closer.

"I suppose you mean to flirt with me?" Caroline looked squarely into his eyes.

"You might suppose that, but I ask what your intention is for me? Do you intend to lead me along, like a kitten to a string? You must come to know and trust me."

"And why must I come to know and trust you?" The music had slowed, and Caroline felt the crowd watching her every movement once more.

Lord Searly paused for a moment and looked more serious as he all but whispered, "I think we shall be great friends."

His words surprised her once more. She shrugged as she passed his side. "I suppose I have been rather severe on you."

He laughed openly. "Yes, yes, I suppose you have, though I am sure I have given you some reason not to trust me."

With that, the song ended, and the couples were lining up for a lively jig.

Lord Searly escorted Caroline to the file of ladies. He tilted his head playfully as he explained, "I must warn you. My jig is quite dangerous."

Caroline laughed genuinely for the first time all evening. "I will take care. I thank you for the warning."

Though the dance did not allow for much talk, the duke's expressions and movements were entertainment enough. The man to the right of Lord Searly had almost taken out the duke twice with his spirited spins and leaps. Lord Searly had given Caroline a pleading look, and dodged the man rather dramatically. The effect left Caroline's sides aching from laughter by the end.

Afterward, the duke escorted Caroline to a seat near the punch, retrieving two glasses. He smiled as he handed one to Caroline. "Perhaps I may steal you later?"

Caroline shook her head apologetically. "My dance card is all but full."

Lord Searly did not look the least deterred as he replied, "What a shame for the poor chap that will miss his dance." And with that, he disappeared in search of his next partner.

It was after the fifth dance, that Caroline sought a seat for a much needed rest.

Lucy appeared out of the crowd and made her way through a maze of people to Caroline's side. "How were your famous dances with Lord Searly?" She had spoken it with pride. "It is too much that you led the ball!"

Caroline's eyes widened as she clutched Lucy's arm. "Yes, it was too much! I felt every eye in the room on me. However, Lord Searly turned out to be quite amusing. I think we shall find a friend in him after all."

"A friend?" Lucy leaned closer to Caroline as she whispered seriously, "Come now, you are not telling me everything."

Caroline hesitated. Perhaps she was attracted to the duke, but her association with the man was so new, and something in her heart warned her to be cautious.

"Ah, there you are, Miss Lucy. Shall we?" Mr. Jenkins said. He held out his hand in invitation.

Lucy accepted Mr. Jenkins's arm, but only after turning to Caroline and whispering, "You must tell me everything."

Caroline nodded, sighing softly. The ball, though enjoyable, was tiring. The forced conversation, the heat, and even the beautiful gown were all beginning to feel suffocating. It was not until a small intermission for the musicians that Caroline saw Lord Searly again. He was scanning the ballroom, searching, his eyes lighting when he spied her. He made his way toward her.

Though Caroline pretended she had not seen him, she could not pretend she did not feel his presence directly behind her.

He spoke in hushed accents, bending toward her neck. "It is a rather nice evening for a walk in the gardens. Do you not agree?"

Caroline spun around, unaware of how close his face was to hers. "May I remind you that I am a lady? I hope you are not suggesting anything scandalous."

"Oh, you imagine too much. It will not be entirely without chaperones. Come, you shall see." Lord Searly turned and walked toward an open terrace. Caroline sat undecided, but when Lord Searly had reached the threshold and stared at her mockingly, Caroline stood and followed the duke out the door.

The terrace overlooked an intricate array of gardens. A small path, out of what appeared to be gray stone, wove throughout the elaborate maze. There were not many lanterns, but the moon was bright and the light from the ballroom illuminated the various trees, shrubbery, and landscapes. The view eased Caroline's nerves, and she silently reflected on the much larger and familiar gardens at Whitefield Hall.

"I do not think I have seen a home in town equal to yours, Lord Searly," Caroline offered in sincere compliment. "The gardens are lovely."

"You must see it in the spring. I have a beautiful rose bush that is particularly alluring." He paused. "I am happy to see everything is to your liking."

Caroline began to tense. Her expression became once again severe as she inquired, "Why must you carry on so, as if you have known me for some time?"

"You do not like the attention?"

"I did not seek it."

"Still, you have once again avoided my question."

"Perhaps it is because I do not know what to make of you."

Lord Searly's face twisted as one of his brows rose in amusement. He pulled his face forward to accentuate his words. "Ask me anything. I will be frank with you. I can tell you are not like most young ladies, set out to trap a duke." He began to laugh.

Caroline was silent. If Lady Hopkins had it her way, that is just what she'd have Caroline do. Caroline pushed the thought aside, resuming her inquiry. "Why have you chosen to pay such attentions to me on such short association?"

"You are different." Lord Searly stopped, staring at the moon. "I was intrigued by you the moment I heard you conversing with Mr. Clark about my riding boots in the window. I sensed your fire."

"My fire?" Caroline looked toward Lord Searly in disbelief, shaking her head. "And so you wish to bask in my flames?"

"To put it shortly, yes."

Caroline leaned against the railing, shivering as she whispered, "But you do not know me."

"Yet. You shall see."

Caroline felt a tingling sensation as he touched a loose curl of her hair. "I have never met a more striking woman, in qualities or looks."

A blush rose to Caroline's cheeks, and she was grateful for the disguise of the shadows. She swallowed hard as she at last found her courage. "I do not trust you one whit, Your Grace."

"And why is that?"

Caroline shook her head in frustration. "Perhaps it is because I see you for what you are, an incorrigible flirt!"

The honesty of her comment must have surprised Lord Searly, for he fell back a step and broke into laughter once more. He shook his head, slapping his hand against his thigh. "Have you not considered that because you see me for what I am, I find you attractive? Surely everyone must have their equal."

Caroline was not laughing. She did not mean to talk so intimately with him, and she sensed Lord Searly had taken her frankness as permission to be even more blunt with her.

Lord Searly reached for her hand, placing it inside his arm. His voice was softer now. "I cannot imagine a more beautiful night."

She nodded, though she did not agree. The only thing different about this night was the moon and the beautiful gardens. She was sure Lord Searly said it only to soften the mood. Perhaps he had grown tired of her distrust. She tried to say something amiable. "I suspect you see many beautiful nights, standing here looking at these gardens. I can only imagine it in spring."

"It is one of the benefits of my birth," he said.

Caroline blushed. His words served to reprimand her for her behavior. She pulled her hand away slowly. Of course Lord Searly was free to be as direct and outlandish as he chose. People would always make allowances for those of such rank and wealth. She cleared her throat. "I almost forgot who I was addressing this evening. You are practically royalty. I am sorry I have spoken so freely. I hope I have not offended you, Your Grace."

Lord Searly turned toward her, his face for once completely serious. "I wish you would forget the title more often. It is liberating to be spoken to with such honesty."

Caroline took a nervous step to the side, pretending not to feel the burning in her throat.

Lord Searly sighed. "It is so refreshing to know you, Caroline."

A cold wind blew up against Caroline. She peered at the moon, now partially covered by a descending fog.

"It is getting colder. Perhaps we should—"

Caroline turned, just as Lord Searly had put one arm to her waist and the other to her cheek. He leaned toward her, his hand lifting her chin to kiss her. She dodged him dramatically, suddenly awakening to her senses. She ducked under the height of his arm toward the opening of the ballroom. She was walking much too fast to be considered ladylike, but she did not care.

She spied her father lazily chatting with Mr. Frandsen and sat beside him, anxiously clinging to his arm. Even Lord Searly would have his limits, and Caroline doubted he would have the nerve to approach her again after such behavior. Caroline tried to tell her heart to calm down, to stop beating so loudly. The perspiration forming at her temples was beginning to slide down her cheeks. She breathed in deeply, suddenly aware of her father's soothing voice.

Lord Hopkins and Mr. Frandsen were in a deep discussion, and Caroline could not help watching Lucy admire the pair. Lord Hopkins, the observant father that he was, cleared his throat, glancing at Caroline. "Mr. Frandsen, I have found your company quite enjoyable. You must visit me in my library so we can continue our discussion, but I am afraid we are boring the ladies with our talk of tenant farmers and estates. Let us not even begin to discuss Napoleon."

Mr. Frandsen grinned. "I am sure you are right, Lord Hopkins. I shall visit you in the coming week."

Lord Hopkins squeezed Caroline's hand. He nodded to Mr. Frandsen, who promptly left his side.

"Caroline, what has you troubled?" her father asked.

But Caroline could not answer his question. Instead, she leaned her head against his shoulder and asked, "Have you ever seen such a ballroom?"

"It is splendid. I hear we owe our invitation to your bright eyes."

Caroline shrugged her shoulders as she mumbled, "I cannot seem to understand why Lord Searly has set his heart upon making my acquaintance. I have been anything but encouraging."

Lord Hopkins scratched his brow. "Perhaps that is why he desires to know you. Some gentlemen are set on the chase of it all. Do not let it cloud your judgment, Caroline."

The music had turned lively again, and Caroline found the moment ironic.

"I fear I will disappoint you, Papa."

Lord Hopkins shook his head, biting the side of his lip. "My darling, nothing could be further from the truth. You are most certainly prepared to make every decision that lies ahead. You have never allowed your mother or me to dictate you. Certainly you will not allow Lord Searly to do so now."

Caroline pulled away from his shoulder instantly, fixing her eyes on her father. "You mean to say you do not approve of him?"

Lord Hopkins let out a large sigh as he grasped Caroline's hand tightly. "I do not mean that at all. Lord Searly is a respectable man. Even more so, he is a duke. He has a great fortune and you could not do wrong by encouraging his attention, that is—unless you did not feel him your equal in heart and mind."

Caroline exhaled slowly. "Papa, I suppose you have ruined me for I shall never meet another man equal to *you*."

Lord Hopkins smiled, pulling Caroline to her feet and dancing with her for the next two songs. Caroline did not even glance at her dance card again.

CHAPTER 8

Lord Searly could scarcely eat his breakfast. He had never been so affected by a lady. Caroline had injured his pride, but instead of feeling bothered by her, he worried he had lost the little gains he had made with her. He left his plate full and went to his credenza to begin writing a letter. His words were open and honest, and he hoped she would see them as such. It was his one strength.

Dearest Caroline,
Allow me to apologize for not acting my part as a gentleman. I fear your beauty and charms clouded my judgment. I forgot myself. I know not how to restore what little trust you had in me, but I will endeavor to prove my worth to you. May I call on you in two days? I will await your reply.
Your humble servant,
Jonathon Searly

Lord Searly penned the address and gave it, along with a single rose from the ball, to be posted directly by the footman himself. The footman was warned of its delicate nature and was entrusted to only deliver it to Miss Caroline herself.

Caroline was sitting in the parlor with Lucy and Miss Kensington when the footman arrived. Upon receiving the letter and token, Caroline excused herself and escaped to her room directly.

She did not want to think about Lord Searly today. Last night had been enough thinking of him to last a while. Caroline read the letter carelessly, tossing it to the side when she finished. The flower lay, untouched and unappreciated, beside her left hand. She refused to admire it, to smell it while pondering the arrogant man. She would wait to reply to his letter. Perhaps a day or two of waiting would do the duke some good. Furthermore, she still felt tired from the festivities. Her feet ached from the exercise.

Her left foot had a large blister from her new slippers. The emerald green slippers were by far the most elegant ones she had ever owned. Small pearl beads had been stitched into the rim of the slipper, with a pale ivory lace ruffle near the top. Caroline had never owned a finer set. She determined it was the rigorous dancing that was responsible for the large infected pinch, though she shook her head in dismissal of Mr. Clark's prestigious skills as a cordwainer. She would have to tell him one day.

The morning turned to afternoon before she knew it, but Caroline remained in her room all day. She had claimed a headache when Louisa informed her Mr. Jenkins had come to call on her and Lucy, and she had pretended to be sleeping when Louisa brought tea and biscuits. Lady Hopkins must have been impatient to see her, for she had knocked on her door three times. Caroline had feigned a snore on one occasion, hoping to avoid her mother's talk of the ball, and more specifically, Caroline's time with the duke.

When Caroline peered out the window and saw Lady Hopkins step into the carriage, she exhaled loudly in relief. Caroline could finally roam the house freely. Yet, instead of running to the kitchens for food, she called for Louisa to help her dress in her riding attire. She felt the insatiable need to leave the house. Only riding could cure this state of mind.

The ride in the park could not compare to Caroline's rides in the country. Even riding in the park was a social affair. Caroline could scarcely ride two minutes at a time without meeting an acquaintance from the ball or concerts. It was not until Caroline began to trot and venture off the path that she felt the crisp winter breeze on her face and began to feel at ease. Her thoughts turned to Whitefield Hall. She missed her little brother. She missed teasing him. Caroline hoped John was enjoying his time away at school, but even more so, Caroline wished John could be there to ride with her now.

Upon spying a fallen tree in the near distance and without a warning to her groom, Caroline took off in a sprint to clear the tree. The jump was executed well, and she stopped to catch her breath. She found herself laughing aloud at the exercise, as well as at the worried look on her groom George's face. He was an anxious old man, and his surprise at her actions always left Caroline amused.

She turned away from him, finally finding her steadiness had returned. To her surprise, she found she was not alone. There, in the shade of a nearby tree, sat Mr. Clark eating a small picnic while reading a book.

George was shouting to her anxiously. "Miss Caroline, you must wait!"

She turned and smiled broadly, alleviating the poor man's anxiety. She then approached Mr. Clark, but he did not seem to recognize her, or, at least he did not acknowledge her. He continued to read his book.

"How do you do, Mr. Clark? It is a bit chilly for a picnic in the park." Caroline was now walking, leading her horse by the reins.

Mr. Clark looked up from his book. His dark eyes were now squinting; his eyelashes casting a shadow on his cheek. He awkwardly rose to his feet, straightening his hair as he did so. "Miss Hopkins, you have discovered my secret retreat. It is a beautiful day, and I was only reading before I returned to my work."

"It is a pretty day, if you'd like to catch a chill. I see you like to read. Anything in particular?"

Mr. Clark paced a few steps, surveying Caroline. He did not answer her question. He simply flashed the cover of the book at Caroline instead. It was the Bible. Caroline nodded in embarrassment. She had caught Mr. Clark in a moment of solitude and reflection. She began to turn away, but Mr. Clark must have sensed her embarrassment.

"I saw you clear the jump. Do you ride often?"

"Yes, of course. At home in Chelmsford, I ride every morning. I find it great exercise."

"You do not find the ladies' mount too tiring?"

Caroline laughed. "Well, yes, it would be more comfortable to ride like a man."

Mr. Clark almost smiled. His lip twitched as he changed the subject. "Are you pleased with your slippers, Miss Hopkins?"

Caroline let out a small laugh as she considered her sizeable blister. "Ah, now I do have a word or two for you, Mr. Clark." She grinned as she gestured to her foot. "I am afraid my left heel has quite the blister."

This time, Mr. Clark smiled. "I am a cordwainer, not a magician. Even the best shoes will raise a blister until broken in."

"So I thought you would say, but are you not renowned for your innovation as a cordwainer? Can you not reach higher than to create shoes as instruments of torture for young ladies dancing at balls?"

Mr. Clark smiled, the small dimple to the right of his mouth rising. Caroline had not understood just how handsome the man truly was until now. "Of course I could do better, but I did not expect you to be dancing the whole of the ball."

Caroline was taken back by the jest. She found her composure swiftly, and patted her horse tenderly. "Did you not? I see. Well, as Lord Searly's particular guest, I found myself dancing the whole evening."

"His *particular* guest? You must be honored, truly." Mr. Clark's face was twisted in a sarcastic expression.

Caroline laughed, shaking her head as she did so. It surprised her to hear him speak of the duke with such humor.

Mr. Clark joined her as she walked toward her groom. "I can take a look at your slippers if you bring them to the shop. Would that suit you?"

"That would be most serviceable, Mr. Clark. I do not know if I can endure this blister for one more ball." Mr. Clark looked amused, but Caroline could not read beyond the expression. She mounted her horse and tipped her hat to him. "Good day to you, sir."

He nodded as she trotted away.

Upon entering the house, Caroline was startled to find Lord Searly and Mr. Frandsen sitting with Lady Hopkins and Lucy.

Her mother must have heard Caroline's footsteps, for Lady Hopkins rushed out of the drawing room entrance and called after her. "Caroline! You are home at last. I did not expect you to ride today after your dreadful headache this morning, but you have been gone for nearly two hours. Are you quite all right?"

Lord Searly had also risen to meet Caroline in the hall. With her face flushed from her exercise and the heat of the riding attire, Caroline felt the surprise might overwhelm her. Lord Searly had not waited a mere day for her reply.

"Miss Caroline, allow me to tell you how well you look." The duke's handsome face surveyed her own. Caroline curtsied but did not meet his gaze.

"Caroline, please, you must change directly and join us in the drawing room. I cannot stand to have you standing here in that dirty dress," Lady Hopkins replied, gesturing for Lord Searly to return to the drawing room. As the pair of them turned their backs, Caroline heard her mother murmur, "Your Grace, you must excuse her. I fear the ball has left her not quite herself. Perhaps the dancing made her a bit dizzy." Caroline heard Lord Searly's polite laughter in response as she climbed the staircase.

Caroline felt her anger rising. Had he really attempted to kiss her? She trembled as she considered her own behavior on the terrace, the questions she had asked. But there was not time to consider her feelings any further. Louisa stood in the chamber, ready to assist Caroline out of her riding gear. Within a quarter of an hour, Louisa had managed to scrub Caroline's face until it shined, pin the loose curls to the top of her head, and fasten the newly purchased afternoon gown. Caroline sat in silence, staring at her reflection. She did not know what she would say to Lord Searly. Not after last night.

When Caroline entered the drawing room, the duke rose to his feet.

"Good afternoon, Your Grace," Caroline offered without the slightest hint of enjoyment.

"Miss Caroline, I called on you today in hopes you would recognize my sincere gratitude for your presence at my ball."

Caroline tried to ignore her mother, who was winking at her encouragingly. "Yes, I see you are quite thoughtful. You must regard the evening as a success, then?" she asked, refusing to meet his eye. She seated herself on the window seat, out of her mother's view. She could not stand for any more winking or eavesdropping.

Lord Searly winced at her reference to the ball. He made his way toward the window, his right hand shaking as he explained, "It was not without its—how shall I put this—difficulties, but I will call it a success for I enjoyed the best of company. I doubt I have had as equal a dance partner as you, Miss Caroline. You must cause quite the uproar in Essex." He smiled warmly.

Lady Hopkins inched toward the couple. Apparently Caroline had not escaped her mother's hearing. "You may depend upon that, Lord Searly. Caroline has always been much admired for her grace and delightful disposition. I would not be surprised if she had stolen many a heart in Chelmsford." She cleared her throat, smiling. "I see you dance quite elegantly yourself. The pair of you dancing was a delight to witness! That's the only way dancing should be done."

Caroline shot a warning glance to her mother, which effectively sent Lady Hopkins to the other end of the room to Lucy and Mr. Frandsen.

Lord Searly watched Lady Hopkins's movement as his voice became a hushed whisper. "Caroline, please speak to me."

"Do not address me so. I cannot understand why you would continue to attempt at familiarity after your ungentlemanly behavior." She whispered, but her voice threatened to rise.

"Forgive me, but it is not entirely my fault. You were much too charming. I fear the punch had stolen my inhibitions." He now sat beside her, his hand stretched toward her.

"And would you have been so apologetic had I not fled your presence?" she replied, finally meeting his gaze.

At that, Lord Searly let out a nervous laugh. "Perhaps not. Still, I did not mean you any harm."

Caroline blinked in disbelief. "Are you not aware of the damage you might have caused me?"

"It might have done your reputation some good, Caroline. I am not such a bad connection."

Caroline dropped her hands to her side in frustration as she retorted angrily, "And that is the only way you suppose to have done me damage? Have you not considered my feelings, my modesty?"

Lord Searly's expression softened. "I have considered only my own feelings. Would you wish me away because of a moment of weakness? It was not as scandalous as you suppose."

Caroline sighed, considering Lord Searly's words. Perhaps she had been overly judgmental. She swallowed hard, deciding whether or not to forgive him. "And you would not wish to be pushed away with such behavior as mine has been? I am sorry. I do not mean to be resentful. I suppose I may have even encouraged your outrageous behavior with my own openness and questions. You must forgive me."

"Caroline, I will not listen to you speak so. The fault was mine entirely. I suppose I wished to lead you astray. Come, let us be friends once more." His sincerity could not be mistaken.

Caroline tilted her head, hesitantly smiling as she assessed him. "I suppose we shall be friends if you will stop sending me notes and flowers."

Lord Searly clapped his hands against his thighs and released a deep laugh. "I shall at last be able to sleep tonight!"

His absurdity left her laughing once again. "I do not think I shall ever understand you. You are quite ridiculous!"

Lord Searly nodded in agreement. "Yes, I suppose I am, but I am thankful you will not hold it against me any longer." He stood from the window seat, smiling broadly, and turned toward his cousin. "Come, David, our work here is done. We must be off and allow these ladies some peace and quiet."

Chapter 9

Twenty-Five Years Earlier

Phillip sat beside his mother as she patted him approvingly on the shoulder.

"You shall do nicely. I could not have asked for a better match. Miss Davenport is just the prize your uncle and I have been hoping for."

Phillip sat uneasily, refusing to meet her penetrating gaze.

She continued to press him. "And why, may I ask, are you so prickly this evening? The affair is already settled, is it not? I thought you approved of the lady."

To this, Phillip pulled away from her, dropping his face to his hands.

"Phillip, stop this ridiculous charade. You should be celebrating your engagement, my boy! It is not every day these things work out so nicely," she explained, crinkling her nose. Her crooked teeth looked exaggerated, and for a moment, Phillip thought she resembled the monster he was beginning to think she was.

His voice cracked as he desperately explained, "It isn't right, you know! The poor girl has no idea what she is marrying into."

Mrs. Hopkins twisted her face in a mocking smile. "Of course she does, Phillip—she is marrying into title and reputation."

"But she does not know the situation of the estate," he said despairingly. "My uncle, he has ruined us. She will see the reason for our match. She will never forgive me."

Mrs. Hopkins only smiled at this, smoothing his coat along the lapel. She gave a slight hiss as she spoke, "Ah, so that is it, is it? You are in love with the girl! My poor Phillip, what better reason than love is there to marry?"

Chapter 10

Twenty-Five Years Later

Lord Hopkins surveyed his wife nervously. He had just questioned her plans for Caroline. Lady Hopkins dismissed his questions and continued to spread jam across her toast.

"Eleanor, you would subject your daughter to a lifetime with Lord Searly merely for the title of Duchess?" He was pleading more than he was asking.

Lady Hopkins exhaled loudly. "I am not suggesting anything of the sort, Phillip. God knows I would never wish my child unhappy. I truly feel they are well suited to one another, and when their infatuation wanes—which is always the case, mind you—she will be better situated than we could have ever hoped for."

Lord Hopkins was silent for a moment, shocked at the words he was hearing. Lady Hopkins sipped her tea, either oblivious to or uncaring of the pain she was causing him.

"Why are you so insistent?" he asked.

Lady Hopkins rolled her eyes and took a bite of her toast.

Lord Hopkins felt his blood begin to boil. He threw the newspaper on the table, while knocking his knuckle against its surface. "How can you be so unfeeling?"

His display seemed to awaken Lady Hopkins from her disaffected mood. Tears filled her eyes. She stood quickly, brushing her skirt with her hands as she walked. Just as she passed the frame of the door, she turned around and spouted, "I suppose you think me as evil as your mother, Phillip. However, I would never dream of selling my daughter for a title the way your mother so carelessly sold you in return for my fortune." She left in haste, ignoring Lord Hopkins's protests and pleas.

Caroline found she had checked her reflection an astounding six times that morning. She had borrowed a yellow afternoon dress from Lucy. The white lace across the bodice was delicate and complimented her complexion. Caroline abhorred vanity, but there she sat, peering into the mirror again while she pulled the lace gloves over her fingertips. She began to pinch her cheeks once more, when she let out a frustrated growl and tossed the small mirror aside. Lucy entered the room just as Caroline was leaving.

"Goodness, Caroline. You look absolutely radiant." Lucy's eyes sparkled as she spoke. "And just where are you off to?"

"I thought I'd go to town this afternoon. After my chance meeting with Mr. Clark in the park, I thought I might take my slippers to be adjusted," Caroline explained.

"Ah, yes, your blister. Of course you should have the slippers fixed," Lucy said, nodding. Then, before Caroline could say another word, Lucy grabbed her sister's arm. "You must let me accompany you, for I too was hoping to go to town this very day."

The bell on the shop door rang, startling the clerk. Caroline watched as the man laid the book down on the desk in front of him, met her near the door, and offered dryly, "Miss Hopkins."

Caroline presented her ball slippers and smiled warmly. "I have brought my slippers for Mr. Clark. He is to adjust them." She attempted to peer around the curtain.

The clerk straightened his glasses. "He is with a customer at the moment. You may wait if you like, or I can schedule a private appointment, at your home perhaps?"

"No, that will not be necessary," she replied, clutching the bundle as she seated herself. "I shall be glad to wait."

The clerk returned behind the curtain, and Caroline waited in silence.

Within ten minutes, the clerk emerged again from behind the booth, followed by a beautiful young lady. She was dressed prettily, albeit in country attire, and her golden curls bounced as she laughed. She could not have been older than eighteen, and Caroline felt her stomach churn as the girl giggled profusely as she addressed Mr. Clark informally.

"Oh, Tom! You must not tease me! I am sure my cousin means nothing but kindness." She startled upon seeing Caroline, seemingly aware of Caroline's intense scrutiny.

Mr. Clark followed the girl, laughing as he walked. He placed his hand on her back, leading her toward the door, but upon seeing Caroline, he pulled his arm back to his side and stiffly said, "Miss Lenore, the boots will be finished within the week."

"Thank you. As always, Tom, good day."

Mr. Clark watched her leave and then turned to Caroline. The ease about him was now lost. He offered a small bow to Caroline, and upon seeing the slippers in her hand, shook his head knowingly. "Miss Hopkins, I see you have come for your fitting. If you will follow me." He motioned toward the back booth, holding the velvet curtain open as she entered the small room.

Caroline thought she noticed the clerk giving Mr. Clark a taunting look, but Mr. Clark did not seem to see it. Instead, he knelt carefully in front of Caroline, examining the small slipper in his hand.

"You are without a chaperone today, Miss Hopkins?"

Caroline blushed at this, but found she replied impulsively. "My sister is across the street. Did not your last customer come unaccompanied?" She looked down at him as she said it.

"Yes, she did come unaccompanied."

Mr. Clark continued to feel the slipper. He gently checked the back of Caroline's left foot, locating the waning blister.

"Was I mistaken, or did you call her Miss Lenore? Was that the enchanting Miss Georgiana Lenore that I have heard so much about?"

Mr. Clark grinned and nodded. "So, you have heard the tales. Yes, that was Miss Georgiana."

Caroline frowned. Miss Lenore was indeed handsome. For all the gossip she had endured from the Jaspers about their precious Georgiana, Caroline had not considered that there might be any truth behind their praise. She swallowed. "Miss Georgiana Lenore is a cousin to my nearest neighbor in Chelmsford. I have heard tales of her beauty and accomplishments for the past four years."

The clerk was talking loudly to a customer at the front.

Mr. Clark's lip twitched. "And now you have seen her in the flesh."

He was marking the slipper with a few pins. "Now," he said, "I shall endeavor to transform this slipper from an instrument of torture." A broad smile now covered his face, but Caroline only sat seriously. He silently replaced her boot. "Your slippers will not take long. It is an easy mend."

She nodded but did not move. When she raised her head, Mr. Clark was staring down at her. They locked eyes for some time, both assessing one another.

At last, Caroline swung her head to the side and asked, "Mr. Clark, are you as friendly to all of your customers, or is it just Miss Georgiana Lenore who has caught your eye?"

Mr. Clark's deep vibrato laughter returned, along with a slightly amused expression. He cleared his throat, his lip quivering as he offered, "Yes, I find I am comfortable with Georgiana."

Caroline felt her cheeks color. He had called Georgiana by her first name. Caroline was humiliated to find herself continuing. "You are well acquainted then?"

"Yes, *very*."

Caroline stood in embarrassment and attempted to leave the booth, but Mr. Clark gently stopped her, a wry smile spread across his face.

"Georgiana is my cousin."

Caroline reddened instantly, astonished at the truth of such a possibility. She nervously inquired, "Your cousin? Why you—you are not related to the Jaspers, are you?"

Mr. Clark's laughter returned. "Do you think I resemble Charles much?"

Caroline shook her head in confusion. No, Mr. Clark did not look at all like Charles Jasper. Charles's thin frame, thinning hair, and protruding belly did not compare to Mr. Clark's dark curls and broad shoulders.

"You cannot be serious then," Caroline said, though it was much more of a question.

Mr. Clark's laughter faded, but his smile remained. "No, I am not related to Charles Jasper in the general sense. Georgiana Lenore is the daughter of Miss Charlotte Lenore, sister to your neighbor Mrs. Jasper. I am related to Georgiana through her father, my own mother's brother."

"I see," was all Caroline could muster. She stood awkwardly at the opening of the booth, tempted to flee.

"And further, do you suggest that I am not pleasant to my customers?" Mr. Clark's voice cracked. Caroline almost thought he was teasing.

"I meant to say, you seem . . . ," Caroline's embarrassment threatened to overwhelm her. She shook her head and smiled, pretending she had meant nothing by her earlier inquiries. "I only meant that you seem to keep your distance. You are, after all, most professional."

But Mr. Clark had seen the look on her face. "I am a serious tradesman."

"Yes, but I see now you are not always so serious. Is it my station? You find my conversation frivolous?" Caroline's green eyes flashed with interest.

Mr. Clark held her gaze, tilting his head as if defensive. "I was not born into title or station. I am neither afforded the time nor the desire to run with the London ton. I hope I do not offend you, Miss Hopkins."

"Perhaps you think me selfish and spoiled?" Caroline asked in haste.

"I did not say that. I was merely pointing out—"

"But you confess you do not socialize with women of my standing?" Caroline dared to look directly at him as she spoke.

"Perhaps you are more fortunate than I have been. I was working at an age when most gentleman you are acquainted with are sent off to school." Mr. Clark turned away from Caroline and leaned against a spare stool.

Caroline shuffled toward him, aware of the tension she had caused. She did not know why she always brought up such questions, for she did not like the answers to most of them. She bit her bottom lip and apologetically lowered her head. She attempted at reconciliation. "I am sorry. That was quite impertinent of me." She paused, exhaling slowly. "How have you come to own such a shop? I know the difficulty that lies in procuring your services. You have made quite the name for yourself and your skill."

Mr. Clark shrugged his shoulders but did not shy away. He looked directly back at her. "It is true I have worked very hard to build my reputation. I left home at the age of fifteen and begged an apprenticeship from a friend of my father's. I assisted him for four years until I had learned all I could from him. I then traveled to Paris and found work at a specialty cordwainer shop. I worked under one of the greatest cordwainers in all of Europe for nearly seven years. It has taken me a long time to become what I am. I do not mean to appear cold. I am only dedicated to my craft. And of course, I refuse to forget where I came from."

"Forgive me," Caroline replied. "I would not presume to question your diligence and discipline. I admit I am spoiled. I have parents that have indulged me ever since I can remember. I have grown up with the many comforts you speak of, but does that make me so far beneath your notice and manners?"

Mr. Clark fumbled with his apron. "I would not rank you beneath anyone, Miss Hopkins. I would venture to say it is your observant nature that makes you so noticed by the likes of Lord Searly."

"But not by a man incapable of frivolities?"

Mr. Clark inched closer. "I did not think you cared for the attention of such men."

His face was a mere foot away from her. Caroline felt her heart quicken. His dark eyes seemed to pierce her. She fell back a step, wiping her gloved fingers across the small beads of perspiration that had accumulated on her brow as the result of her nerves. "It is not that I seek attention, but rather that I be considered an equal to those with real substance. Can you not see the offense that blatant disregard might cause?"

"Blatant disregard?" Mr. Clark scratched his chin in disbelief. "I have attended to you as a customer in a satisfactory manner, have I not?"

She was doing it again. Caroline reeled her head backward in frustration, commanding herself to act more pleasant. "Most satisfactory, I suppose, except for the large blister on the back of my foot," she said lightheartedly.

Mr. Clark's shoulders relaxed.

"Mr. Clark, I suppose I must endeavor to be less frivolous, while you must endeavor to be a little more. You cannot be so serious at all times. Do you not enjoy dancing and concerts?"

"Of course I enjoy a good dance and good conversation. You think me primitive?" Mr. Clark inquired as Caroline unintentionally began to laugh again. "I spent many evenings in Paris dancing."

The front bell rang loudly. Two customers were waiting. The sound caused Mr. Clark to search for his watch. "I must attend to my work," he said, turning toward Caroline.

"Of course. Thank you, Mr. Clark. Good day."

Thomas continued to clear the drafting table that had become cluttered with notions throughout the day. He bristled past Joseph dismissively, setting the crate down beside the table.

"Your cousin seemed in a good mood today. Have you asked her about me?" Joseph was leaning against the table.

Thomas sympathetically glanced at Joseph. The poor clerk was nearly twenty-three, and vastly inexperienced when it came to love. Joseph had sworn he had fallen in love with Georgiana at first meeting, two weeks ago. Joseph attempted at fashion, but with fiery red hair, a prominent nose, and small spectacles that balanced across the brim, he was not what most considered handsome. His attire made him appear much older than his twenty-two years. Further, Joseph had maintained his bookish ways from being away at school. His manner was rather odd.

"I would not become so enamored with a girl like Georgiana. She is young, ambitious, and infinitely silly." Thomas swallowed. "It is no use, Joseph. She will only be satisfied with a fortune and title."

Joseph shrugged, his gaze falling to the floor as he clapped his hands together softly. "Oh, I had never really believed she was the girl for me, at least not in the realistic sense."

Thomas was sure his clerk was disappointed. "You must go out dancing, Joseph. There are other pretty ladies that are not quite so silly."

Joseph let out an uncomfortable laugh, straightening as he said, "I think I shall try my luck with another girl. What about you, Tom? Miss Hopkins looked very pretty today."

Thomas felt his composure slightly weaken at the mention of her name. "I think many consider her handsome."

Joseph let out a high-pitched chuckle. "But you do not?"

Thomas looked at the clerk seriously, and with only a hint of humor replied, "I do find her pretty, yes, but it is not her figure or face that catches my eye."

Joseph lifted a hand in confusion. "Then what impresses you about the lady?"

Thomas smiled. "I've yet to figure it out."

Chapter 11

"Caroline, you have truly outdone yourself!" Lady Hopkins exclaimed as she strode into the room, her arms outstretched.

"Mama, I'm not sure I catch your meaning," said Caroline, clenching her jaw.

"Darling, you must not tease me so. The whole of London is talking about you and Lord Searly. You have captured his eye, but have you captured his heart?"

Caroline's turned away, unsure of how to respond. "I suppose he has paid me great attention, but I cannot presume to have captured his heart. He is quite a flirt, Mama, and I would be foolish to suppose he meant anything by his attentions to me." Caroline stood and walked to the piano.

"Caroline, you must see that love always has a beginning. Lord Searly may not be serious yet, but I feel he is in great danger of falling in love with you. You are just the sort of girl that he needs."

Caroline sighed exasperatedly. She pulled her hands to her temples, shaking her head. "Why ever would you say such a thing, Mama? We hardly know the man! To presume I am compatible with the duke on such little acquaintance—"

"Do you really feel we know so little of him?" Lady Hopkins interjected. "I feel his attentions to you at the ball spoke measures of your potential match. And, when you were gone a few days ago, he waited nearly forty minutes for your return. Lord Searly is a man of great regard, but he has shown you the greatest consideration. His eyes follow you, and while he is courteous to me and our family, it is you he desires to be acquainted with." Lady Hopkins was waving her arms in a rhythmic pattern to emphasize her point, but stopped when Caroline shook her head in frustration. Lady Hopkins fell to the seat of the piano beside Caroline, softening her tone. "You cannot be indifferent to him, can you?"

Caroline's fingers grazed the top of the keys, producing a scattered melody. "I am not indifferent to him, Mama. I am flattered by his attentions. He is handsome and wealthy, and agreeable. Yet I feel there is a side to him we do not know. Perhaps I only need more time."

"That is perfectly understandable, my dear. I would not wish you unhappy simply for the connection. Though, I do hope you will understand the significance of such a union. It would be such a comfort to me to see you happily situated. You have a fortune in your own right, and I think it fitting you found someone similar in that regard. You cannot know what it is like to be pursued solely for your fortune."

Caroline caught the sadness in her mother's voice and placed her hand lovingly on Lady Hopkins's shoulder.

Lady Hopkins, suddenly aware of her daughter's scrutiny, smiled broadly and clapped her hands together. "But to be young again! I shall never forget the romance. Your father was so charming. He knew just how to compliment a lady, a trait he still exhibits often." She paused, shaking her head in reverie. "I remember how my heart raced each time I saw him." A smile crept across her face.

"I hope I shall be as lucky, Mama," Caroline whispered.

Lady Hopkins stood abruptly, leaving Caroline alone at the piano to practice.

CHAPTER 12

Twenty-One Years Earlier

Lady Hopkins stared solemnly at Lord Hopkins. He had not answered her question. She repeated it, her voice shaking less the second time.

"Did your mother have you court me because of my fortune?"

Lady Hopkins had overheard her mother-in-law conceitedly discussing the matter with one of her pompous friends.

Lord Hopkins's eyes were misty, and his voice trembled as he recalled, "Eleanor, you must believe me. Perhaps in the beginning, it was so, but after I came to know you, it was all so different—"

Lady Hopkins shook her head in disbelief and left his side before he could finish. Her small hands flew to her growing belly, and the cries she had suppressed while in her husband's presence began to echo down the hall.

CHAPTER 13

Twenty-One Years Later

Caroline was surprised one morning when she left the breakfast room in search of her mother, only to find Lady Hopkins standing in the parlor with Lord Searly. The two were speaking on familiar terms and in hushed voices. Caroline watched her mother touch the duke's arm more than once, laughing politely at his teasing.

Her appearance disturbed their comfortable conversation at once. Lord Searly straightened immediately, taking a step toward Caroline. He gave a low bow, awaiting Caroline's hand, which she reluctantly offered.

Lady Hopkins smiled warmly at the display, her hand against her cheek in reverie.

Lord Searly was the first to speak. "Caroline, you are looking well this morning."

Lady Hopkins sighed, unaware of her volume.

Caroline pulled away feebly as she entered the room. "I did not expect you, Your Grace. What can your purpose be in calling at this early hour?" she asked directly, staring at her mother instead of the duke.

Lord Searly softly chuckled and shook a finger at Caroline. "I see I cannot put a thing past you, my dear. I should hope you would be happy to see me, whatever the hour or reason." He paused, now pacing around the room dismissively. "However, if you must know, my footman was delivering invitations to a small dinner party I am hosting, and I was already set to pass by your home. I determined to deliver it myself."

Lady Hopkins was enthusiastically smiling as she nudged

Caroline's side. "Can you believe the duke, delivering the card himself? Have you ever heard of such a thing?" She giggled in satisfaction.

Lord Searly returned the smile and playfully responded, "I would never dream of such degradation, were it not for the fine ladies I find here."

Lady Hopkins teasingly swatted her hand at him.

Caroline absentmindedly tapped her fingers across the table beside her.

"Oh!" Lady Hopkins exclaimed with wide eyes. "I have just forgotten to instruct Betsy on my new dresses!" She left the room without another word.

Caroline eyed Lord Searly suspiciously. "I had not thought you on such familiar terms with my mother."

The duke strode toward Caroline. He lifted his arm to touch a stray strand of her hair, just as he had the night of his ball. "One does what one must."

Caroline retreated to the sofa, realizing Lord Searly had planned an extended morning call.

He sat beside her. "I only wanted to be sure of your attendance at my dinner party."

Caroline nearly choked. "You did not think my mother would refuse a chance to socialize with a duke and duchess, did you?"

Lord Searly laughed openly. "Certainly not, but I want her to like me."

Perhaps it was the awkward silence that ensued, the uncomfortable look on his face, or the surprise of the morning, but all at once, Caroline broke out in laughter. She found it was futile to resist his teasing, and he, seemingly aware of her displeasure of finding him so, laughed in relief that she had finally given way to his attempts to smooth things over once again.

It was evident that Lady Hopkins was anticipating the event. In the days that followed, Caroline overheard her mother gossiping of the possibilities such an invitation suggested to any and all that would listen. Her friends, upon hearing such news, had each validated her suspicions and begged Lady Hopkins not to forget them when the family was connected to such nobility.

Caroline felt overwhelmed by her mother's expectations and had looked to her father for comfort, but found he provided even less consolation. Lord Hopkins, in contrast, could not be induced to see anything positive about the invitation. Whenever Lady Hopkins or Caroline visited the topic, he turned sluggish, only willing to offer a slight "hmmm" or groan. Caroline only wished she knew what *she* felt about the ordeal.

When the day and time had finally arrived, the Hopkins family arrived punctually and in style. By eight o'clock the family was seated at the large table. The company included Lord Searly, Lady Searly, Mr. Frandsen, the Hopkins family, three additional gentlemen, and two ladies whom Caroline had never met before.

The four-course meal was more excellent than anything Caroline was accustomed to at Whitefield Hall, and by the time the desert biscuits arrived, Caroline felt the seams of her stay threaten mishap. The dinner was lit by candlelight and the meal was nothing short of divine, but the conversation had moved along at a painfully slow pace. Lady Searly had directed most of the discussions. The old duchess had spoken only a few words to Caroline during dinner, spending most of her time accosting Lord Hopkins with inquiries into his ancestry and estate in Essex. Lord Hopkins had openly responded to all of her questions, only pausing to suppress a smile when Lady Searly asked about his family's history of infectious diseases and birth abnormalities.

It was made clear to the entire Hopkins family that Lady Searly did not consider this a friendly dinner party, but rather a test of pedigree.

Lord Searly, seated next to Caroline, was unusually quiet. He only spoke in an effort to redirect the conversations to more lighthearted topics, an effort not unnoticed by the duchess. She consequently ignored his attempts and continued in her uncomfortable talk.

At last when dinner had ended, Lord Searly assisted Caroline out of her chair. "I am afraid my mother is resolved to find out every detail of your ancestral line."

Caroline glanced at him curiously when he spoke, unaware that he still held her hand. "I suppose gossip and pedigree could be interesting if one had a reason for knowing it. Does she have a reason, Lord Searly?"

The duke only grinned.

It was when the ladies were excused to the sitting room, that Lady Searly seated herself beside Caroline. The duchess smiled elegantly, if not a bit condescendingly, and began conversing with Caroline. "Jonathon speaks very highly of you. Are you accomplished?"

Caroline smiled politely, albeit secretly bothered by the duchess's effort at conversation. "I am afraid I am not as accomplished as you would wish. I play the piano and sing in the confines of my own home exclusively. I neither sketch nor paint, and I am by no means bookish."

Lady Searly crinkled her nose at this. She held an elaborately painted fan in her hand and had begun wafting it gently. The old woman leaned forward. "Is there nothing you are good at?"

Caroline's eyes widened in surprise and found she could not swallow the uncomfortable laughter that escaped her lips. "I am a gifted horsewoman, and my mother also tells me I am gifted with a needle and thread."

Lady Searly licked her dry lips. "So you ride and embroider? That is what you offer my son and his title?"

The impertinence of the woman rendered Caroline speechless. She had known Lord Searly to be blunt and forward, but Caroline had never imagined as much from the duchess. Caroline furrowed her brow. "Lady Searly, I am afraid you are mistaken. I do not offer your son anything."

The duchess was now staring at Caroline with what Caroline could only guess was contempt.

"He has never asked as much, and I can assure you I have not considered the matter, for we only met four weeks ago."

Lady Searly rolled her eyes and furthered her uncomfortable speech. "With spirit like that, I can almost assure you my Jonathon will develop some sort of feeling for you. It is only unfortunate that you are not highly accomplished. The true importance lies in the example you set for your children."

Caroline felt as if the heat of the room might overcome her. Never had Caroline been confronted so forcefully, and by someone she had just met. She feared that responding to the duchess might cause offense. So, a simple nod and polite smile was all she offered.

It was a comfort to Caroline that the gentlemen arrived quickly, filling the room with chatter and laughter. Lord Searly challenged Lord Hopkins to a game of chess, and Mr. Frandsen began a lengthy conversation with Lucy and Lady Hopkins. The old duchess, to Caroline's relief and surprise, claimed a headache and retired early, leaving Caroline content to roam. She spent some time perusing the books on the table, most of which held little interest. She then paced the room, examining the gold-trimmed furnishings and intricate antiquities.

It was near the end of the evening when Lord Searly approached her. "Your father has wounded my pride. I have not been defeated in that game for nearly two years."

"Papa has always been a formidable opponent." She smiled, staring into Lord Searly's brown eyes, noticing they lacked their usual gleam. "Are you feeling all right?"

Lord Searly relaxed his shoulders and attempted a flirtatious smile. "How could I be anything but happy while in your presence, Caroline?"

Caroline glanced around the room, certain he had been overheard, but the rest of the party was distracted with the games and lively chatter. "Lord Searly—"

"Jonathon," he corrected her.

"Is nothing the matter? You seem preoccupied?"

The duke shifted his weight again, silent for a moment. "Indeed I am preoccupied. Has my mother been awfully brash? I cannot doubt it, for she always is. Something about her rank seems to give her the idea that she can say whatever she wishes to whomever she wishes."

It seemed to Caroline that both the son and mother subscribed to the idea. Caroline attempted to ease his mind as she shook her head, but Lord Searly's piercing gaze broke her composure. She began to laugh.

Lord Searly shook his head knowingly. "I probably warned her five times not to speak to you. I told her it would ruin my chances."

Caroline ignored this, examining the portrait over the fireplace. "That portrait must be of your father. Is it not?"

"Lord William Jonathon Searly," he said formally, gesturing toward the painting. "It is a good likeness of him. The artist caught his *exact* expression." The duke's countenance fell, and he continued in hush tones. "He has been gone for seven years now."

"You must miss him."

"I am required as a son and gentleman to agree with you, though I cannot lie to *you*, Caroline. He was not an affectionate father, and I doubt he spoke more than two words to me, except to criticize or dictate."

Caroline continued to stare at the portrait and found herself critiquing the man. "He does not look like a man that is easy to approach, but he does have an air of elegance. He was a handsome man. You share his likeness, but I think you do not share his stiffness."

When she turned to Lord Searly, he was intently studying her. "I would hope you would not find me stiff. Pray, tell me, how do you find me?"

The blush on Caroline's face would not seem to fade as she searched her mind for an appropriate response. "I have not come to a conclusion of your character yet. At times, you have proven a shameless flirt and a hopeless tease without a trace of propriety, but I am sure there must be more to you than that." She bit the edge of her lip as she pondered a moment more.

After a moment of silence, Lord Searly erupted in laughter. "You must not think too hard about it. You have described me better than my own mother would."

Caroline swallowed. She knew at least one thing about Lord Searly. He was incapable of being serious.

The duke must have sensed Caroline's thoughts, for when the Hopkins family departed, he caught Caroline's hand as she was about to step in the carriage and whispered tenderly, "I am most serious in my attentions to you, Caroline."

She steadied herself, feverishly climbing into the carriage.

Chapter 14

Thomas set the boot down, refusing to acknowledge his cousin's request.

"Tom, please! You must come. If I am to endure my aunt and cousin, I must have you there," Georgiana pled as she grasped his arm.

"Georgiana, I cannot see how my presence would help," Thomas picked up the boot again and began shaping the leather with his strong hands.

"But your acquaintance, Tom, is sought after. Your reputation precedes you wherever you go. There is no one that is above your notice. Even my aunt adores you. Think what a distraction and relief you will be to her and to me." Georgiana began to pout, sticking out her bottom lip.

"I do not like being valued because of my skill."

Georgiana laughed aloud. "I do not value you for your skill, cousin. I value you for your directness and dancing!"

Thomas sighed, knowing Georgiana always got her way. "I will be there, Georgiana," he replied, and while trying to hush her squeals, added, "Now go, so I can work in peace!"

Georgiana gathered her belongings, almost skipping out the door. She turned, exclaiming, "I shall not complain again of my brothers being so far away, for I have the dearest cousin to take their place!"

Caroline was sitting in her favorite garden at Whitefield Hall, the sun shining bright and the birds singing softly, when—

Louisa's hurried movements in the chamber startled Caroline, the dream vanishing instantly. Caroline shot up, scratched her head, and tried to remember the pleasant scene. Louisa carried with her a handful of clothes and placed them at the foot of the bed.

"Miss Caroline, I am sorry to wake you, but it is nearly noon. You must dress. You have company coming within the hour—Mr. Jasper and his mother." She smiled mockingly, then left in a hurry from the room.

Caroline slipped back under the covers. *Surely this is a bad dream*, she mused.

However, it was not long until Louisa returned with a small tray of tea. The maid began sorting through Caroline's dresses and plucked a white frock from the closet, staring at Caroline and tapping her foot.

"Must you be so impatient? I have just awoken, Louisa!" Caroline cried.

To this, Louisa began to chuckle in a deep, heaving manner. In a scornful tone she said, "Yes, I suppose you have just awoken, while I have been up a good six hours."

Caroline sat up, glaring across the room at her maid.

"Yes, you can look at me all you want, young lady, but I am not leaving till you are good and ready for company."

Caroline finally sighed loudly and pulled herself out of bed. She allowed Louisa to poke and pry at her until, at last, the maid smiled in pride and patted Caroline's back.

"Now, have a bit to eat before your company arrives."

Caroline shook her head. She had lost her appetite at the thought of seeing the Jaspers.

The maid said nothing, but she shook her head in, what Caroline could only assume, was disapproval. Louisa had worked for the Hopkins since Caroline was a young child. And though Louisa could not be more than forty years old, she looked much older. Her gray hairs now shone through the blonde, a fact Louisa attributed to Caroline, and the wrinkles around Louisa's eyes filled Caroline with mystery. The maid did not talk much, but Caroline knew there was not much that escaped Louisa's watch. Her hearty laugh, escaping only too often in the presence of Caroline, was a sound that Caroline found strangely comforting.

Caroline discovered Lucy in the drawing room. Lucy was situated in the corner of the room with her knees beneath her, reading a small book. Caroline crept behind her sister in silence and took a seat near her. Lucy was enthralled with her reading, troubling herself only to move when turning a page. At last, Lucy closed the book, exhaling deeply as she held the book to her heart.

"Was it that moving?"

Lucy jumped from her seat and stood, glaring at Caroline.

A small smile snuck across Lucy's face. "It was, actually, and Caroline, if you insist on sneaking up on me, I shall have to find a more private place of reflection!"

Caroline smirked as she saw the book of poetry. "Oh dear, Lucy. I had not thought Lord Byron capable of such reflection."

Lucy gave a swift glance at Caroline, pursing her lips. "I suppose that is because you lack the depth of understanding."

Caroline smiled and nodded, though both knew Caroline's studies far surpassed those of Lucy's. Caroline came to Lucy's side, holding her arms out in surrender. The two embraced and had just began to confide in one another when the clock struck one and Lady Hopkins entered the room followed by Mrs. Jasper, Charles, and Louisa, who was holding a tray of tea.

"Mrs. Jasper, may I inquire about your health?" Lady Hopkins asked cordially. "You look well. How do you find town this year?"

Mrs. Jasper fidgeted with the lace on her sleeve, while lifting her chin to the air. She tilted her head and twisted her petulant features into what some might consider a smile. "I find town has been pleasant enough. I daresay my niece has proven to be a favorable relation. Oh, how she dotes on me! Why, just the other day, she asked me to go to town with her to meet her famous cousin, Mr. Clark. Georgiana treated me with a tour of the shop, and I was permitted to see the man at work. It was most entertaining. I cannot begin to imagine a more remarkable young man," Mrs. Jasper replied as she eyed Charles.

Caroline sat in silence, composing multiple replies and questions in her head for Mrs. Jasper. The woman had, as always, turned a simple question into a discourse on her precious niece, while also making everyone else in the room feel uncomfortable.

"I am sure Miss Lenore does you credit. I am sure she could not have a more gratified aunt." Lady Hopkins said, smiling as she brought a cup of tea to her lips.

"Or a more gratified niece," Lucy added.

Caroline nodded. As usual, Lady Hopkins and Lucy always knew the right thing to say.

Charles looked tense. His eyebrows seemed to furrow more with each word Lucy spoke. He was studying her with even more scrutiny and attention than usual.

Caroline finally cleared her throat. She smiled the best she could and inquired, "Have you found many diversions, Charles, since we last spoke?"

Charles dropped his gaze from Lucy immediately, turned toward Caroline, and strode along the room's length with his chest extended in a horribly overstated manner. "I am not the type to carouse around the gaming scene, if that's what you mean." He attempted to sit in a gentlemanlike fashion, yet his bad posture was only exaggerated more. "I do have news, and perhaps an invitation, if Miss Lucy, that is, if you both would . . . find it acceptable?" His pitch rose as he spoke the last phrase. Saliva had gathered at the corners of his mouth as it always did, while his eyes fixed on Lucy.

Mrs. Jasper put her hand out, impeding him from continuing. "What Charles is attempting to convey, Miss Lucy and Miss Caroline, is that we would be honored by your presence at a small party next Thursday evening at seven o'clock. It will be a party of youngsters like yourself—a few games, lovely refreshments, the like . . . you cannot find it a disagreeable way to spend the evening, I daresay." Her eyes narrowed in a threatening manner.

Caroline swallowed the lump that was now forming in her throat as Lucy smiled appropriately.

"But of course, Mrs. Jasper. They would be most delighted," Lady Hopkins replied with a warmness Caroline could not even pretend to feel.

The sour expression on Mrs. Jasper softened as she relaxed her shoulders, winking at Charles candidly. For his part, Charles secured Lucy's hand and bowed exaggeratedly. With no more than a few exchanges, the odd mother and son were gone, leaving Caroline and Lucy to discuss the unfortunate occurrence.

Chapter 15

Lord Searly sat tall in the saddle. It was a cool February morning, but a good day for riding nonetheless. The duke questioned Caroline about Whitefield Hall and her brother, John.

Caroline's cheeks were colored from the wind beating against her face. She lifted a hand to her head to steady her riding hat as she attempted to answer the duke's inquiries. She told him more than she had meant to, but with each answer she offered, he listened quietly, only asking another question in response. She told him of her home, the small brook at the corner of her family's property, and the tall trees that she often climbed as a small girl. She indulged his curiosity. She spoke of John lovingly, disclosing how she missed him while he was away at school, how she and he liked to tease one another. Caroline had never seen Lord Searly so attentive. Only periodically did he chuckle to himself.

When they rounded the southwest corner of the park, Caroline saw the duke repeatedly eying George. "Is there a reason you watch my groom so intensely?"

He nodded as he quipped, "Caroline, you have me again! I don't know how you do it." He pulled his horse to a stop and dismounted.

Caroline stopped, confused, but followed suit.

"Shall we take a stroll?" He gently motioned to a small clearing by some trees.

After the groom had caught up to the pair, Lord Searly handed George the reins, while offering Caroline his arm. The couple strode along the frosted ground in silence, until finally Lord Searly spoke.

"It is a lovely day." He turned toward her, a mischievous grin spread across his face. "Though I do confess, I do not think it would be quite so lovely without you."

Caroline cast him a reproachful glance, but did not pull away. "I do not know why you must always ruin the moment with that shameless talk."

He placed his hand on hers. "I find it amusing to tease you. The way you furrow your brows in disapproval is nothing short of adorable."

Caroline shook her head. "You speak of me as if I was your pet."

Lord Searly stopped, and with forceful sincerity he caught her gaze. Caroline's eyes darted away, glancing around nervously. She had seen that look before. To her surprise, Lord Searly had led her to a private enclave. The groom was still in sight but not in a position to see them clearly.

"Caroline, I must speak frankly. You must see your power over me."

Caroline attempted to pull her hand away as she felt anxiety sweep over her. "Power over you? I am not a sorceress."

"Ah, but you are, my dear. You have bewitched me with your beauty, your stubbornness, and your passion. I cannot see a way out of this one."

Caroline stared blankly at the man. *A way out of this one?* She tore her arm from under his and crossed her arms in front of her. "I do not see your meaning. I have never intended to trap you, Your Grace."

He let out a hearty laugh as he helped her to a small bench. "I do not think you ever attempted to trap me, a refreshing change from the rest of the lot. I found you charming and pleasant at first, my amusement for the season, I decided. But then . . . but then you have been so different from any other woman I've met. I simply will not be content to let you go."

Caroline felt her cheeks darken in blush as she turned her head away from him. She cleared her throat, stumbling over her words, "Lord Searly, sir—that is, Your Grace, how can you talk so? What you speak of is, is—a silly phase that will end just as the season."

Lord Searly reached for her face, softly brushing her cheek and cupping her small chin in his hand. "Are you so indifferent to me?" His face was serious, and Caroline could sense the deeper man once more. "Please, tell me if I have no chance."

Caroline bit the side of her cheek, shaking nervously. It was the same question her mother had asked of her. She was not blind to the man's charm. She met his gaze once more, replying with a tremble in her voice, "No, Lord Searly, I am not indifferent to you."

His eyes brightened as she spoke the words, but his reply startled her. "Then shall I speak with your father?"

Caroline sprang to her feet, placing her hands on her hips. "No, you mustn't!" she shouted. She was startled by the rapidity of her own words. "That is—I am not ready for anything of that sort. I cannot give you any promise as of yet. I feel I am—I am afraid I require more time."

Lord Searly knelt before her on the melting snow. He stole her gaze once more and calmly whispered, "I shall wait for you."

Chapter 16

Thomas pulled the cravat from his neck and flung it on the floor despairingly. If his father could see him now, he would have shaken his head in shame. To have worked so hard and attained so much, only to be defeated by a cravat! Thomas flung himself on the bed, and forced himself to breathe deeply. At long last, he returned to the silky heap upon the floor, determined to do his worst to the poor thing.

His reflection was the picture of a gentleman, but Thomas felt like an imposter. His fresh navy coat had only been worn three times this season, and his elegantly tied cravat had been the result of countless hours of battling. Thomas did not feel at ease in such attire. If it were not for Georgiana, Thomas was sure he would have spent the evening working. She was like a sister to him. And though Thomas had acquired the status of a gentleman because of his skill and Georgiana had become a much sought after lady because of her looks, Thomas knew they shared something much deeper—their upbringing. They knew what the bottom looked like, and they had both taken the opportunity to rise above it.

Georgiana welcomed Thomas into the Parlor. After being greeted by Mrs. Jasper, Georgiana's insufferable aunt, and Charles, Georgiana's cousin, Thomas found he was the last to arrive in the company. He nodded cordially to the faces he did not recognize, resting on the face of Miss Caroline Hopkins. He smiled genuinely, and offered a slight bow. Georgiana took his arm, leading him along.

"I must introduce all of you to my dear cousin, Mr. Thomas Clark. He is the renowned cordwainer of London, but more importantly, the dearest friend to me. This," she said, turning to Thomas, "is Miss Margaret Bolton. We met when I was away at school. She is a dear soul. To her left is Miss Cora Crawford, a friend of Margaret's. Then there is Mr. Smith, Mr. Low, Mr. Jenkins, and the young Hopkins girls—Miss Lucy and Miss Caroline, both of whom I am honored to come to know. You, of course, have already met my aunt and Charles."

Thomas nodded politely, hoping he would not be quizzed on the first five names Georgiana had mentioned.

Georgiana beamed up at the others. "You must excuse Tom. He may seem shy, but just wait until you see him sing or dance!"

Thomas scowled as he found a seat near the three gentlemen. He could feel Caroline's eyes following him, and he could not help stealing a look at her. She looked beautiful, in a light green evening gown, her dark curls cascading down the back of her head. A gold chain hung from her slender neck. Her eyes seemed to brighten as if she was pleasantly surprised upon seeing him. She met him with a smile, and Thomas found he was at a loss for words. He stumbled as he attempted to address her.

"Miss Caroline, Miss Lucy, you—you both look well this evening. I presume you have enjoyed London?"

They both smiled, but before they could answer, Georgiana interrupted. "Come now, Tom. You did not tell me you knew any of my guests! Pray, how do you know the famous Miss Lucy and Miss Caroline Hopkins?"

Thomas raised one brow. "They are my customers. Did you forget you have crossed paths with Miss Caroline once before?" he asked, his eyes fixed to the floor.

Georgiana sat in silent contemplation for a moment.

Miss Bolton brightened and turned to Lucy. "Truly? Miss Lucy, you must tell me how you managed it! My mother has attempted to procure me an appointment with Mr. Clark for ages. I have only recently had my measurements taken, thanks to Georgiana." She smiled in admiration at Thomas.

He shrugged off the attention, attempting a stroll around the room.

"I'm not sure, Miss Bolton, though my sister and I are aware of the talents and reputation of Mr. Clark," Lucy replied sweetly. "He has already completed our ball slippers. We now await new boots."

"I am simply sick with anticipation of my new slippers," Miss Bolton said, swooning in Thomas's direction.

"You best take care, Miss Bolton," Caroline interjected with a hint of mockery. "I had a sizable blister at the back of my foot after wearing my slippers the first night. I would not wish it upon you."

Thomas chuckled, but refused to join the conversation. He picked up a few encyclopedias that lay on a side table and began flipping through the pages. The ladies continued to chat openly, while the three other gentlemen sat listening. Charles, Thomas noticed, stood strangely close to Lucy, staring down any gentleman that dared to look toward her. Lucy looked most uncomfortable situated so closely to her neighbor, yet she continued in her sweet manner, conversing with the other ladies.

Thomas had not joined in much of the conversation. In fact, he had almost removed himself entirely from the company, when he heard Georgiana break into a whisper. However, it was the kind of whisper that was more audible than hushed.

"Miss Caroline, I have heard so much about you. We have hardly spoken, but I am excited at the prospect of becoming more acquainted. Tell me, is it true what they say about Lord Searly having his attentions fixed on you?"

Caroline blushed at the mention of Lord Searly's name, and Thomas felt uneasy. She attempted to answer Georgiana in hushed tones, but Thomas caught her response below the others' ramblings.

"I would not believe everything you hear, Miss Lenore. I do not think Lord Searly has serious intentions with any of the ladies he meets." Caroline sat taller, straightening her gown.

"But he does flirt with you, then? He is so handsome, and so rich! I've heard that he is the catch of all of London!"

Caroline inched closer. "Miss Lenore, you must forgive me. I cannot speak for the man. I suppose I amuse him, yes, but there is little substance beyond that between us."

Georgiana sighed loudly. "I only wish I could meet him. I have seen him twice in town, once at a ball where he nodded to me. I thought I should faint of heat. He is supremely elegant. I do not know how you talk about him so dispassionately."

Caroline smiled, but did not respond further. After a moment of pause, she prompted Georgiana loudly, "Did you not say your cousin Mr. Clark is an excellent singer?"

Georgiana giggled as she turned toward Thomas, who was now standing much closer to the pair. "Why yes! He is excellent. He must sing for us tonight." Georgiana stood, motioning to Thomas, and made her way to the piano. Thomas followed her, while giving a marked glance at Caroline.

"And without the slightest protest?" Caroline said with a smile. "Very well, Mr. Clark, for if there is anything I abhor, it is false modesty."

Thomas shook his head playfully, but made no reply. It was pointless to protest when Georgiana was so insistent. She began playing a soft melody, one of which Thomas and her had sung together often. It was a song his father had taught him when he was a boy. The room fell silent as he began to sing, and his rich baritone voice seemed to fill the entirety of the room.

Thomas dared to glance at Caroline. She had moved closer to the music stand, resting one hand against the bookshelf. She appeared to be equally moved and surprised by his abilities. When she saw him looking at her, her eyes quickly darted downward and she took a step back to the settee. Mr. Clark finished the last note and escorted Georgiana to her seat. The small group applauded heartily.

"Bravo, Mr. Clark!" Miss Bolton exclaimed, a little too enthusiastically for Mr. Clark's taste. "You are not only a gifted cordwainer, but also a supremely talented singer."

"You put us to shame, Clark. I shall not get even a glance from the ladies, now," Mr. Low lightheartedly proclaimed.

Thomas nodded graciously.

"Mr. Clark, I must ask," inquired Miss Bolton, "How did you come to sing so beautifully?"

Thomas shrugged his shoulders as he turned toward the inquisitive faces. "My father sang. We used to sing together. I spent seven years in Paris, and while there, I learned the art of being a gentleman."

The three other men began to laugh.

Mr. Low placed a heavy hand against Thomas's shoulder. "You must teach me this art. I suppose it might help my efforts with the ladies."

A few giggles erupted.

Thomas seated himself across from Caroline.

Miss Bolton, Lucy, and Miss Crawford followed with solos on the piano. It was pleasant enough, but Mr. Smith had had enough. After Miss Crawford had been applauded and sufficiently complimented, he stood and addressed Georgiana. "Miss Lenore, shall we not liven up the evening with a few games?"

Georgiana brightened at the suggestion and nodded approvingly. "Perhaps we shall! And I know just the game to start it off." She proceeded to blow out the candles in the parlor, squelching any light to be seen, except for a single candle she held near her face. From behind her back she pulled out a crimson scarf.

"Who shall be first in blind man's bluff?"

Charles jumped at the opportunity. "Count on me, cousin!"

Thomas heard Caroline stifle a small giggle, and Lucy looked relieved at the absence of Charles from her side.

Georgiana commanded Charles to bend to his knees while she fastened the scarf around his eyes. "You all know the rules, yes? Charles will be blindfolded as we move around the parlor. He must catch one of us and correctly guess who he has caught."

Everyone nodded. Even Thomas knew the game. And with that, the small group was shuffling around the room, attempting to avoid the uncomfortable reach of Charles.

Thomas was quick to dash behind the drapery. He hoped to steer clear of all the action. He peeked from behind the drapes and watched the others scurry across the room.

Caroline was pressed against the nearby window, and Charles was approaching her. His lanky arms scattered all sorts of trinkets around as he clumsily searched every surface for any sign of human flesh. Sure of being discovered, Caroline dodged a swing of his arm and ran almost directly into Thomas behind the curtains.

"You have discovered my refuge, Miss Hopkins," Thomas softly whispered.

"I shall endure any confinement to escape the grasp of Charles Jasper."

Thomas accidentally laughed. "And that is the only enticement worthy to confine you with a man such as me?"

"I suppose I would venture behind the drapery with you often if it meant you would sing to me," she replied. "An enticement I'm sure Miss Bolton would not object to, either."

Thomas shook his head, raising a brow at her, though he knew she could not see it in the darkness.

Their quiet conversation was interrupted with a slobbery sound from beyond the drapes. "Lucy? Is that you?" Charles's arms were moving up and down the drapes now.

Caroline was forced to move closer to Thomas. The two were silent as Charles continued his search. He reached behind the drapes, and in desperation, Caroline retreated directly into Thomas's chest. Thomas twitched upon the encounter, but afraid of being discovered in such a situation, remained motionless. At last Charles's searching hands seemed to concentrate in another direction. Caroline retreated in an instant, too embarrassed to say anything.

It was then that Charles's hand magically reappeared, the muffled sound of "I have got you at last!" making its way to Thomas's ears. Caroline attempted to fly to the other side of Thomas in order to avoid the flailing arm when she hit her head against the marble mantle with great force. Thomas caught her by the waist as she fell unconscious to the floor.

CHAPTER 17

Caroline woke to a pounding headache. She felt her mother's hand holding her own. Before she even opened her eyes, she knew it was morning. She heard the birds chirping just outside her window. Usually a delightful sound, the birds' songs now sent a stabbing pain behind her eyes. She cringed at the noise, pulling the covers above her head.

"Caroline? Are you awake?" asked Lady Hopkins, her voice full of concern.

"Yes, Mama," was all Caroline could muster.

An elderly woman spoke, "Drink this, child. The peppermint will do your head some good."

Caroline lowered the covers and opened her eyes slowly, only to find she was not in her own room. She sipped the herbal concoction obediently, willing to drink anything so long as it offered relief from the headache she now faced.

"What happened? How did I—" Caroline looked to her mother questioningly.

"You took a blow to the head last night. Do you not recall anything?"

"I remember hitting my head, but—where am I?"

"You are still at the Jaspers' home, I am afraid. The doctor did not think it safe to move you, for fear of bleeding in your brain. You hit your head quite hard. Mr. Clark sent for Dr. Rose, and then for me, as soon as it happened. Bless his soul. The doctor will return in a couple hours to check in on you."

Caroline tried to sit up, but found the task quite impossible. "Oh, Mama. I do not want to be a bother, even for Mrs. Jasper."

"Hush, Caroline. I will hear nothing of it. I am just glad to see you awake and speaking in coherent sentences. You were talking quite the load of rubbish last night." Lady Hopkins dabbed at Caroline's head with a cold cloth.

Caroline's eyes widened. "What did I say?"

Lady Hopkins's smile seemed to brighten the dim room. "When Mr. Clark carried you to this room, you yelled that you were quite well enough to walk yourself. When we tried to pacify you, you began sobbing, begging to see your Papa."

Caroline cringed at her mother's words, shaking her head in disbelief. She gripped her mother's hand tighter. "That is dreadful. Is that the worst of it?"

Lady Hopkins smiled playfully but did not answer. "I think it best if you get more rest before the doctor arrives."

Dr. Rose diagnosed Caroline with a concussion, one that he felt optimistic she should recover from easily. He did advise, however, that she not be moved from the Jaspers' home until she showed no signs of trauma. It was impossible to tell the extent of the damage, but Dr. Rose cautioned those commissioned with her care to be watchful for any strange behavior.

Caroline felt utterly out of place at the Jaspers. Though there was little she could do about the situation, she could not help wishing she was anywhere but there. She was burdened with Mrs. Jasper's frequent visits, during most of which Caroline feigned sleep. Occasionally, Georgiana would appear to check on her. Luckily, Charles was not allowed in the room.

Lucy had promised to visit daily, and Caroline felt ashamed to think she was the cause of her sister's having to visit the Jaspers so often. Louisa had come to tend Caroline, which offered only mild comfort when compared to the fact that she was under the same roof as Charles. Furthermore, Louisa was constantly concocting an herbal remedy for Caroline to try, and while some proved effective, others were nothing more than a stinky tea she was forced to drink every hour.

After four days, Caroline felt only a dull headache, which was just what the doctor had hoped for. She felt well enough to sit in bed. She even attempted to read, which unfortunately only led her headache to a relapsing sting. There was little to do but think, and Caroline could not turn her mind away from Mr. Clark. She well remembered his song and their flirting behind the drapery, and she felt humiliated. She had inconvenienced the Jaspers and ended Charles's party.

By the fifth day, Caroline begged Louisa to help dress her. The Jaspers had gone out on this particular day, and Caroline felt the need to escape the bedroom she had been so confined in for the past five days. With Louisa's help, Caroline managed the stairs. Louisa found a small chair and moved it to a back sunroom, where Caroline sat for two hours straight, feeling the sun on her face and thinking of the time she could once again move freely without the stabbing pain behind her eyes. She had almost drifted off as she sat in the chair, daydreaming peacefully, when the chime of the front door interrupted her thoughts.

"If you will just follow me, sir. You may see her yourself."

Caroline shot up in her chair, resulting in a sharp reverberation of her skull. She gripped the sides of her temples, attempting to regain her sense of balance. She lifted her eyes to the doorway to see Mr. Clark. The sight of him startled her so much that she attempted to stand.

"Miss Caroline, you sit," commanded Louisa without the slightest hesitation. "You have a visitor. Take it easy, child."

Caroline nodded as she held her hand out to Thomas. "Mr. Clark, how kind of you to visit. Your cousin has left for the afternoon."

Mr. Clark took her hand, giving a slight bow. "So I hear, Miss Hopkins. How are you? You look much better than the last time I saw you."

Caroline reddened at the mention of the house party. "I feel I must apologize, Mr. Clark. I should have taken more care. I hope I did not disturb you terribly or ruin your evening."

Mr. Clark began to laugh. "Are you truly apologizing for hitting your head?"

Caroline began to relax. She smiled for the first time in days. "I suppose it is silly to apologize for such a thing. Though I confess, I am quite embarrassed about the whole situation."

Mr. Clark nodded his head, and seated himself on a bench nearby. "I hope you are feeling better. What does the doctor say?"

"Oh, I am quite all right, nothing to be so concerned about. I think I should be more concerned about my behavior. Mama says I was talking nonsense the night it happened. What did I say, besides begging for my Papa like a little child?"

Mr. Clark leaned toward her, likely examining the colorful bruise that had spread across her forehead. His eyes fell upon the scab across her hairline. Caroline was pleased it had started to heal at least.

"Oh nothing horribly strange, but you did ask me to sing to you."

"You cannot be serious?" Caroline asked in bewilderment.

He broke into an authentic laugh, his dimple becoming even more prominent. "No, I am only teasing. You did not say much that I could understand, actually. You had all of us concerned."

Caroline sighed in relief.

They stared at one another in silence, until Caroline at last found the words, "Thank you, Mr. Clark, for assisting me that night. I know you sent for my mother and the doctor. I am indebted to you."

"It was all that I could do."

Caroline cleared her throat. "How is your work?"

Mr. Clark looked grateful for the change of subject. "I have kept busy this season. With the likes of you and your sister and Lord Searly as my patrons, the whole of London has sought my craftsmanship."

Louisa had drifted to sleep on a nearby chair, and she erupted in a loud snort, interrupting the chatter.

Caroline and Mr. Clark broke into laughter. The effect of it sent a sharp pain to the top of her head. Caroline sunk to the chair, catching her head in her hands. Mr. Clark attempted to steady her.

"Your chaperone is quite effective," he managed sarcastically through the laughter. "Perhaps this is my signal to leave you to your rest."

"Perhaps you are right. Thank you, Mr. Clark for calling. I am grateful to you for your service to me. I—I feel silly when I think of what happened."

He waved his hand dismissively, replying, "Please, Miss Hopkins, do not mention it again. If anything, I feel at fault for not preventing the accident. I was, after all, invading your section of the drapery."

Caroline was laughing again, so much so that she lost her balance once more. Mr. Clark was at her side, grasping her hand within seconds. Her laughter stopped as she felt the tingling sensation rise up her arm.

He was watching her. "I must go. You are not well. May I assist you to your room?"

She smiled at the offer but did not want him to think any worse of her. "That is thoughtful, Mr. Clark, but I do not wish to involve you in such scandal."

Mr. Clark bent low. "I am afraid I do not catch your meaning. You are unwell. It is nothing to help you to your room."

Caroline was not well. She did long to lie down.

"Very well then, but let us be quick about it." She wobbled as she attempted to stand on her own. He lent his arm to her, which she all but clung to. He patiently assisted her up the stairs, making it a point to only offer more support when she required it. After she had found her footing at the doorway of her bedchamber, Mr. Clark dropped his arm.

"Will you be all right from here?" he asked.

She nodded drearily. He stood at the doorway, watching as she made her way to the bed. "Take care, Miss Hopkins."

With that, he was gone, and Caroline was left alone to contemplate the man.

Chapter 18

Lord Searly had spent the last week in anticipation followed by disappointment. He had called on Caroline shortly after their ride in the park, only to find she was not at home. On further inquiry, he discovered she had fallen during a childish parlor game and sustained a concussion. The fact that she was recovering at the Jasper residence made matters even more frustrating. He did not know these Jaspers, and the idea of parading in, without being invited, left him feeling like a fool. He hoped she would send him word, but after a week, he had heard nothing. At last, he sat at his credenza and inked a short note, sending it along with a small bunch of flowers, as was his way.

Dearest Caroline,

I pray you are making a full recovery and that I may call upon you next Tuesday. I have missed your reproaches.

Yours,

Jonathon

Caroline read the card twice, tossing it to the side of the flowers like she had done the last time he had sent such a card. It was nearing spring, but the late February temperatures were still cold. She did not know where Lord Searly had found such a bouquet at this time of year.

"Caroline, they're lovely. How thoughtful of him." Lucy scanned the bouquet, resting her hand on a large pink blossom.

"Yes, the flowers are lovely," replied Caroline, but she was not looking at them. Instead, she searched her sister's face. "Lucy, I hope you have not been unhappy visiting me here. I know how Charles scarcely allows you a visit without harassing you with his awful talk. I am sorry."

Lucy's attention to the flowers faded as she seated herself by Caroline. "It is not ideal, but my daily visits are worth it to see you. Charles will always be Charles, I suppose. Besides, Dr. Rose is optimistic you will be well enough to return home in another few days." Lucy fiddled with Caroline's hair as only a sister might do, twisting the frays up into the mess on top of Caroline's head. It was not until Caroline began to inadvertently yawn that Lucy decided to return home, commanding Caroline to rest and stay down.

Lucy descended the staircase in haste, hoping to avoid Charles, for Charles had made it a habit in the last week to await Lucy's descent each day. He never had much to say, but he seemed to have a way of postponing Lucy's departure in the most aggravating of ways. First it had been a stanza of poetry that he demanded her intellect to decipher, another day he called her to the parlor to assist his mother in a card game, and on Lucy's last visit, he had asked her for her opinion about the weather. She had replied quickly that it looked like rain, which sent Charles in an awkward state of offering for Lucy to stay for dinner and wait out the storm.

It was too much for her, and she feared his growing interest would only amount to one thing, a proposal. Charles Jasper had always treated Lucy in a particular manner, even as a child. He had once walked all the way to Whitefield Hall to ask her what her favorite flower was. She was only seven then, Charles almost seventeen.

The Hopkins family had always felt it their duty to treat their neighbors with the greatest regard, no matter how taxing they might be. And so it was no surprise that Lady Hopkins demanded Lucy and Caroline always graciously accept Charles's invitations to dance or to attend a party. However, Lucy had grown concerned that all of the congeniality she had been brought up to exhibit to a man such as Charles Jasper might be confused for something more substantial.

Lucy skirted past the parlor door, stopping only to fasten her cloak and bonnet.

"Lucy, I had not heard you were in. What a fortuitous moment."

Lucy turned, squinting her eyes in an unconscious irritated fashion. "Mr. Jasper, I had no intention of disturbing you or your mother. Caroline is doing much better. Please send my regards to your mother." She shifted her weight toward the door, but was surprised when Charles lunged forward, leaning across the opening in anticipation.

"Lucy, I must speak privately with you. Will you join me in the parlor?" His eyes were pleading, and Lucy felt the urgency in his voice. She searched her mind for some excuse, *any* excuse, but could not find a realistic or honest reason why she should not stay.

"Of course. Though I warn you, I must not be long. My mother is awaiting my return."

Charles held his arm to her, and she drudgingly took it, feeling as if the wind had been knocked out of her. He led Lucy to a small nook by the front window. She seated herself, and he stood before her.

"We have known each other for some time, have we not?"

Lucy cleared her throat. "We have. I have always considered you a neighbor and a *friend* of our family."

He nodded, missing the emphasis Lucy had placed on the word *friend*. "And am I correct in assuming I may confide in you?" Saliva gathered at the corner of his mouth, and as he licked his lips, he patted down a small patch of recently sprung hair on his balding head. Lucy turned away, fearing her disgust might reveal itself upon her face.

"You may always confide in me, Mr. Jasper, though I warn that I may not prove helpful to you." She held her hands tightly together, attempting to dismiss the tension she felt.

"I find I am confounded with what action I must take. It is a delicate situation, and as such, I find I must have a delicate woman's opinion of the matter." Charles was now hunched over her, perspiration forming near his temples.

Lucy stared back blankly as she tried to form a sentence in response, but when she failed; she simply nodded, urging him forward.

"There is a young lady, of whom I have known for quite some time, that I have always been expected to marry."

"And may I ask who has expected this match?"

"My mother and I have not always anticipated the union, but it has been the expressed wish of the lady and her mother. And, as I have considered the union, I find it pleases me above all else."

Lucy felt her heart slow to a normal pace. She smiled at last. "What is your obstacle, Mr. Jasper? If it is the desired outcome of both parties, I do not see your need of help from me. You must proceed as you see fit." She attempted to stand, but Charles was there, his sweaty palm pressed against her cheek.

A sudden surge of nausea encompassed Lucy.

Charles leaned in close, spitting as he whispered in her ear, "I have awaited this day in anticipation since the moment you danced with me at Whitefield Hall two years ago."

The action could not have taken Lucy more off guard, and she removed his palm with great force. "Mr. Jasper! Surely you have not been referring to *me* as the woman of your desires?" She looked at his face, attempting to swallow her nerves along with his repulsive behavior.

"Lucy, you must not play the modesty card with me. I have known your mother and you have wished this marriage for some time. I myself heard your own mother urge you to dance a reel with me that night. Your compliance and the regard you have shown to me ever after have convinced me of your affection. And who could blame you? I find we are well suited, and I am determined to make it so."

Lucy shook her head in disbelief. She felt her head burn hot as she attempted to reply calmly. "Mr. Jasper, you have been mistaken. It pains me that you have been misled. If my mother had urged me to dance with you, it was only as a neighborly gesture. As for myself, I have never desired anything more than to be your friend. I pray you will forgive me, but I must leave."

Charles stood, his jaw dropped in agony, as if he had just been punched. His crooked front teeth protruded as he hissed, "You cannot be serious."

"I am most serious, especially when I say it pains me to offend you."

Charles began pacing clumsily, his arms flailing up and down. "And is this sudden change of heart due to one of your new London acquaintances, hmm? Mr. Jenkins, perhaps? I should have thought you above the fickleness of the ton, Lucy Hopkins!" He was yelling now.

Lucy closed her eyes, and breathing deeply she all but whispered, "Mr. Jasper, I have never held affection for you. London has not changed me on that account. I have simply only ever considered you a neighbor and friend. Please, I must return to my mother."

Charles had gone redder in the face, and his eyes were beginning to bulge. His surprise at once turned darker, and he straightened his coat. "You will not get away that easy. I will have you for my wife, even if—" He pulled her into an embrace, placing a slobbery kiss to her neck.

Lucy screamed, slapping Charles across the face. He stood stunned, while Lucy hurried to the door.

"Mr. Jasper, I regret the civility I so attempted to show to you. You disgust me, and I shall never be your wife." She slammed the parlor door and left the home as quickly as her legs would take her.

At the sound of the door and shattering porcelain, Mrs. Jasper ran to the parlor, only to find Charles in a sobbing heap above a broken teapot.

"What on earth has happened, my darling boy?" She knelt beside him, placing her hands on his shoulders.

Without looking toward her, Charles hissed, "She has refused me."

Mrs. Jasper let out a curdling laugh. She nodded unabashedly, "Oh, Charles. There is more than one way to make the girl marry you."

Chapter 19

The last days of Caroline's stay at the Jaspers' home was especially tiresome. She felt recovered, despite the dull pain that appeared upon moving too quickly. Lucy had not visited the last three days, and by the tone of the short letter she had received two days ago, Caroline suspected something had gone awry between Charles and Lucy. Caroline's suspicions were only confirmed when she observed a sharp change in Mrs. Jasper's behavior. The aging woman did not say but a few words to Caroline at a time, as if Caroline offended her or as if Mrs. Jasper had suddenly found Caroline beneath her and Charles's company. Caroline did not mind the slight, for solitude was preferable to the gossip of Mrs. Jasper and the unintelligible ramblings of Charles.

Georgiana, however, did visit with Caroline on two separate days for the whole of the afternoon. Caroline enjoyed spending time with Georgiana. Georgiana had only been sent to school four years ago by the generous and adoring Mrs. Jasper, and there was much of Georgina's manners that schooling had not changed. She was at times outrageous, though she was unaware of her inappropriate ramblings.

Georgiana spoke of her home, her father and brother who leased land from a larger estate to farm. She had grown up working alongside her brothers and sisters at harvest time. When Mrs. Jasper had offered to pay for her to attend a prestigious school, Mr. and Mrs. Lenore were only too grateful to send their daughter in hopes of giving her a brighter future. Georgiana had since become an accomplished painter, and she seemed to radiate contagious enthusiasm.

Caroline found herself laughing alongside Georgiana, gasping at her silly ideas and sympathizing with her anxieties about the future. But, it was Georgiana's talk of her cousin Mr. Clark that captured Caroline's attention the most. Georgiana spoke of him with such affection, such pride. Caroline giggled at the amusing stories Georgiana told of his youth.

It was with great relief that Caroline watched Louisa finish packing her trunk. For the first time in what felt like weeks, Caroline had taken care in dressing. Louisa had fixed her hair into a charming arrangement. The bruising had faded almost entirely and the scab on her forehead had now healed. And so it was, when Caroline's carriage had arrived, she watched with anticipation as the footman loaded her trunk. She offered her thanks to the Jaspers, kissed Georgiana on the cheek, and happily stepped into the carriage.

"I do not know how you bore it." Outrage filled Caroline's heart. She attempted to relax her clenched jaw, but the thought of Charles Jasper assaulting her sister prevented it.

Lucy neatly folded the embroidery, discarding it in her lap. "It has weighed me down. I have never held high regard for Charles, but I never had thought him capable of attempting such ungentlemanly behavior. He was so angry at my refusal." Lucy shook her head violently.

"I cannot bear the man. You should have called for help, Lucy."

Lucy remained silent, small tears pooling in her hazel eyes. Caroline rushed to her side, offering a warm embrace.

Lucy nearly choked as she explained, "I cannot help feeling that this is far from over. He threatened as much—"

She was interrupted by a forceful shake of her shoulders as Caroline's eyes filled with determination and concern. "You will not ever speak to that man again. Do not let him occupy your thoughts, for he deserves none of it."

With that, Lucy fell back into Caroline's arms, sobbing heartily.

CHAPTER 20

Mr. Clark stood, fidgeting with the bundle in his hands, as Caroline entered the parlor. Her eyes lit up when she saw the package.

"I hear you have something for me, Mr. Clark," she said excitedly.

"Miss Hopkins, I had finished your boots some time ago, before the party at the Jaspers', but with your recent . . . I thought it best to wait until you were wholly recovered to call on you with such a trifle. I have also brought your slippers." He held his arm to her, and she took it willingly. After seating himself beside her, he handed her the package. Caroline pulled back the paper scraps to see the boots. She held one out, examining its craftsmanship. The boot was made of smooth leather, stained to a dark mahogany shade. The side of the boot had embellishments within the leather, and Caroline traced her finger along the pattern.

"They are beautiful. Are you sure they are for everyday wear?"

"I'm not sure what else you would use them for." He smiled, taking the other boot from the box. "Shall we try them on? I suppose the fit is more important than the fashion?" He knelt in front of her, and quietly removed the slipper from her foot.

"I'm not sure Lucy would agree with you. I think she has told me numerous times that fashion comes before comfort."

Mr. Clark only raised his brow to her comment as he cinched up the laces. He held the footed boot in his hand, a small look of satisfaction appearing across his face. After both boots were on, Caroline stood and walked across the room.

"I think they fit rather well, Mr. Clark. I am sure you hear it often, but I will say it again. You are talented."

Mr. Clark grinned. "I am glad you like them Miss Hopkins, but I am more pleased that you seem to have recovered so well."

Caroline nodded, finding she could not look away from his dark brown eyes until he bent to collect the paper scraps and box.

"I visited with Miss Lenore on occasion while at the Jaspers'," Caroline said. "I learned quite a few stories about you. I'm afraid your serious manners cannot fool me now. Georgiana told me how you used to pull her hair and wrestle with her brothers. I had not thought you such a tease."

Mr. Clark's shoulders straightened as he turned to face Caroline. "Georgiana was always one to talk. I suppose she told you all sorts of other lies. I will vouch for none of her stories, except for perhaps the ones she told of my honor, bravery, and discipline," he said with a crooked smile.

Caroline brought her hand to her cheek as she pretended to contemplate. "I am not sure I remember such stories, but I will have to ask her when we meet again."

Mr. Clark inched closer as he mockingly added, "Perhaps you'd best not. I would hate to challenge Georgiana's recollections. The female sex can be so sensitive when it comes to matters of memory."

Caroline pursed her lips, standing on her toes to meet his gaze. "I am sure that is correct, in the same way that gentlemen embellish the noble traits about themselves."

Mr. Clark shook his head. He sarcastically explained, "I am sure a true gentleman would never venture to embellish his talents or traits, just as a true genteel woman would never exaggerate the truth."

Caroline nodded, though she did not smile. Her thoughts had wandered elsewhere. She cast her eyes downward, biting the edge of her lip. "I hope you will not find me impertinent, but I cannot forget the situation surrounding my accident. I hope I did not seem . . . ," She colored as she searched for the correct word.

Mr. Clark grinned. "Like you were enjoying yourself?"

Caroline sighed lightly. She crossed her arms and stuck her chin up. "No, that is not what I was I was going to say. I did enjoy myself." She paused, swallowing. "Very much so. I only hope I did not appear unladylike."

Mr. Clark hadn't even a moment to respond when Bentley appeared at the door, announcing the arrival of Lord Searly. Caroline instantly fell back a step from Mr. Clark, her composure crumbling. At this, Mr. Clark's face turned a slight shade of red and he straightened his shoulders. He silently nodded to Lord Searly.

"Lord Searly, I had not heard you arrive." Caroline stood frozen.

There was a slight pause as Lord Searly eyed her, Mr. Clark, and the wrappings in Mr. Clark's arms.

"Good afternoon to you, too, Caroline," Lord Searly replied.

Mr. Clark's eyes were fixed on the bouquet of flowers Lord Searly was holding at his side. "Lord Searly, you find me on a delivery to Miss Hopkins," Mr. Clark said as he held out his hand.

A small smile spread across the duke's face as he shook the outstretched hand. "Clark, I had not expected to see you here, but it is a delight nonetheless."

Caroline found her lips incapable of moving. She only glanced back and forth at the two men in front of her, wishing she could escape to another room, or anywhere else for that matter.

"I had not had a chance to deliver Miss Hopkins's boots until this afternoon. I am just on my way." Mr. Clark turned toward Caroline with a slight bow. "Miss Hopkins."

Caroline followed him past the door, accidentally brushing shoulders with the duke. "Mr. Clark. Thank you for mending my slippers as well. They are lovely, as was our visit," she offered, scanning his face.

"You are most welcome. Good day," Mr. Clark replied much too formally. He turned to leave, and before Caroline could add anything else, he was gone.

Lord Searly took her arm, escorting her back to the parlor where they sat beside one another.

"Caroline, you left me without any word. I called twice on your mother to inquire about you myself." He was seated much too close for her comfort, and his possessive tone seemed unwarranted.

"I did not wish you to worry," Caroline said, avoiding his gaze. "I did not think you would worry. It was but a slight head wound, nothing to be so concerned about."

"But how could I not worry? And with the outlandish circumstances, how could I not wonder? Is it true you injured yourself in a game of blind man's bluff?" Lord Searly looked down at Caroline with furrowed brows.

Caroline felt the heat rise to her cheeks as she was reminded of that night. "It was a silly way to injure myself, but such things happen."

Lord Searly exhaled loudly, and took her hand in his. His voice became exaggeratedly serious as he spoke. "Promise me you will not be so foolish again. I cannot have you hurt. You must realize how I suffered."

"And just how did you suffer?" Caroline asked him blatantly. The way he had turned her suffering into his own was too much to bear.

He straightened. "The thought of you hurt, without me by your side, it was far more taxing than you realize."

"So I am to only injure myself when you are near?" she asked dryly, shaking her head in bewilderment.

Lord Searly laughed. "I would rather you not go about hurting yourself at all, but if you must, then yes, I prefer it if I am there to see to your needs."

What audacity, Caroline thought to herself. She stood, strolling to the window as she watched a carriage drive by slowly.

"Caroline?" Lord Searly asked tenderly.

She did not answer. The only sound in the room was the carriage outside the window.

"Caroline, it is only because I care for you that I talk so." He was standing behind her now, and he ventured to touch her shoulder.

Caroline turned. She felt the anger rising to her face, and before she could calm herself she thoughtlessly exclaimed, "Oh? Is that why you treat me like a child?" She pushed away from his touch. "I think it is time you took your leave, *Your Grace*."

Lord Searly's eyes turned dark at her words, and he twisted his head to the side silently. Caroline was certain she had offended him for he turned to leave without saying another word.

Lady Hopkins was standing in the foyer when Lord Searly came out of the parlor. She smiled warmly at him. "Lord Searly, what a pleasure to see you."

He bowed politely, but he did not meet her gaze. "As always, Lady Hopkins." His voice fell flat, lacking its usual enthusiasm. He cleared his throat. "I find I have come at a most inconvenient time, and as such, I am on my way." He began to collect his hat and coat from Bentley.

"Oh, but you must stay, for it looks like rain, and I have been longing to inquire about your dear mother. How is the duchess? Come, let us visit." Lady Hopkins gestured toward the parlor.

Lord Searly glanced through the open French doors, and upon seeing Caroline's back turned, he shook his head softly. "I fear I must go."

Lady Hopkins sighed sadly. "Your Grace, I hope you will forgive Caroline. She has not been herself."

The duke met Lady Hopkins's gaze at last.

"It has been quite taxing for the poor girl to stay so long with the Jaspers, away from her family. And though she has recovered well, I fear she has not yet recovered from the humiliation of it all."

He exhaled, nodding gently. "I suppose you are right. Thank you for speaking so candidly. I shall make it a point to act more sensitive concerning the matter."

Lady Hopkins grinned as he offered another bow upon his departure.

CHAPTER 21

Thomas had not been able to rid himself of irritation. What was at first surprise and embarrassment had quickly turned to anger and something far worse. He balked at his misery when he recognized the dreadful feeling. *Jealousy*. To be jealous was, of course, not the type of emotion he was accustomed to; and further, to be induced to such a feeling by the sight of Lord Searly and Caroline seemed foolish. Of course the two were suited. He stared at his reflection in the small mirror on the table with a mix of emotions—anger, jealousy, and, most pronounced, pity. He pitied himself. He pitied the fact that he had been so careless as to allow himself to feel something for Caroline.

The whole situation was most unusual for Thomas.

And yet, Caroline was unusual.

Thomas had become enamored with her. He knew she was uncommonly pretty, but the images that sprung across his mind when contemplating the girl had far more to do with the meaning behind her dancing eyes and marked glances. Caroline's green eyes ignited a spark at the slightest hint of humor or debate. Her mind was too quick in processing the mere movement of the brow, an indication of irony, or the slightest clue of hypocrisy. And then, there was the matter of her lips. She smiled far too frequently in comparison with other London ladies. She teased. And yet, when matters became most serious, or better yet, when people concealed their innermost thoughts or feelings, Caroline would pry and ask the most ridiculous questions.

Somehow, Thomas had come to admire Caroline for her courage to question. She questioned everything. Even when Thomas had been conversing easily with her, he found Caroline's eyes were always filled with inquiry as she scanned his face and movements. What answer she longed for, he could only guess, but Thomas had persuaded himself more than once that she longed for his answer of affection. He laughed aloud at the thought. He held regard for a true lady, the daughter of a baron and an heiress of a fortune.

But it was of no matter. He saw everything a bit more clearly now. He saw it would never be. For not only was Caroline of greater rank and financial superiority, but she was above him in intellect and manner. Thomas decided he would find a way to push his feelings aside.

Unfortunately, this resolution did little to change his heart. He found he still contemplated her despite his determination. He replayed their secret display behind the curtain over and over in his head. He remembered the thrill he had felt as she had instinctively sprung to his chest in avoidance of Charles's lanky arm. He became absolutely miserable when he remembered the way her head leaned against his shoulder when he had carried her after the accident. His mind became a hopeless mess of sentimental ponderings—her bright eyes, her laughter, her surprised expressions, the way her tiny hand felt against his arm, her dark curls that bounced as she floated across a room. It was in humiliation that Thomas found himself expelling a loud howl of irritation.

The sound of Joseph's hurried footsteps sent blood rushing to Thomas's cheeks.

"Tom! Are you all right?" the clerk asked seriously. Joseph leaned against the table with a hand extended in the air as he tried to catch his breath.

Thomas twisted his hands in awkward attempts, motioning to the heap on the floor. "I cannot find anything to my liking!"

Joseph nodded. He looked to the floor at the heap of crumpled pages, the hint of a smile spreading across his face. "And may I ask what you are referring to?"

Thomas shook in embarrassment, impulsively knocking a chair over.

"Everything."

Chapter 22

Mrs. Jasper had contemplated the matter long enough, and she felt she had come to a satisfying arrangement. She knew Charles was not the ideal candidate to carry off such a plan, but beggars cannot be choosers. Her only son would marry well, and Miss Lucy Hopkins was the only reasonable choice. The poor girl had refused his polite offer.

"Now, Charles, you must quit this despicable display. You have an upcoming proposal to attend to, my son. You must positively quit this sulking," she commanded, stroking his cheek in a brash manner, albeit tender in her consideration.

"You seem too sure of it, Mother. I do not think Lucy will come near me, let alone agree to marry me." Charles dropped his shoulders and spastically sent his arms flailing, cursing as he did so.

"Charles, Lucy is not beyond persuasion. I feel that given the choice of scandal or marriage to you, she will choose marriage. She is a sensible girl," Mrs. Jasper replied with a look of concern. "At least she seems to be."

"But how is it done? What will you have me do? I do not see how—"

Mrs. Jasper held her hand up in protest. It silenced him in an instant. "I have it on good authority the Hopkins sisters will be attending the spring ball. I have already secured your invitation. You must compromise Lucy in a public fashion if she persists in refusing your offer."

"And what tactics am I to employ in such a venture?"

Mrs. Jasper shook her head in frustration. "Oh, dear boy, by whatever method it takes! I see I must once again dictate your every move."

Charles stiffened, casting his eyes toward the floor. He tapped his finger in contemplation, humming a horrific tune.

Mrs. Jasper exhaled angrily, grasping at his hands in a frustrated fashion. "Oh, Charles. You will never get the girl if you carry on so. And to think you had thought a proper proposal would do the job." She began laughing in condescension. "Charles, you see, life is only full of so many opportunities. If you allow Lucy to slip through your fingers, you will not have such an opportunity for years to come. You must see that, as I certainly do."

"Yes, Mother," he said, a hint of sadness evident in his voice.

"And to ensure you will *not* fail, I tell you this. I have kept it from you for quite some time, hoping you might never need know, but your father's will is very specific, Charles. If you are not married within a year, everything will go to your cousin Felix. If you do not wish to marry a girl you do not know or care for, you must not fail."

Charles eyes widened.

"You see, my dear boy, it is just as imperative to you as it is to me that you marry, and marry quickly. Our livelihood depends upon it."

Charles began sweating profusely. His face reddened as he stuttered, "I shan't fail, Mother. With your help, depend upon it."

Georgiana swallowed hard as she anticipated discovery from behind the doorway. She shuffled around noisily, entering the room in a disheveled haste. "My dear aunt, what on earth could have you both so enthralled?"

Mrs. Jasper waved her arm in dismissal to the question. "Have you seen to your dress for the ball next week, my darling girl?" she asked Georgiana lovingly.

"Almost," Georgiana lied, "but there are few matters I must attend to in town today."

"Of course, Georgiana. Anything you need." Mrs. Jasper grinned.

The shop was filled with the tinkering of tools and Georgiana's chatter.

"Tom, you should have seen the vile woman. Poor Miss Hopkins has no clue as to her impending doom."

Thomas stood in contemplation, holding a carved last in his hand. "Georgiana, you know you must warn her."

"But how? How am I to approach her? Are you not friends with Miss Caroline Hopkins? I am sure she would listen to you. Oh, Tom, it is just that—I feel my loyalties are being questioned. I know it is not right, what my cousin is plotting, but the Jaspers have funded my education, taken me into their home. Somehow it feels like a betrayal to expose them."

Thomas remained silent.

"You must sense my difficulties."

After another bout of silence, Thomas stirred. "Georgiana, the only difficulty you face is one of conscience."

Georgiana shrunk away from him, leaning against a stool.

"I do not mean to chide you, only to remind you of the importance of what you witnessed. Do you not think it was providence that placed you there to overhear your aunt's scheme?"

Joseph entered the booth, motioning to Thomas. "Mr. Lyleton is here for his fitting, sir."

Georgiana straightened her shoulders, glancing to Thomas in farewell.

"Thank you, Joseph," Thomas said softly. "I will be with him momentarily."

Georgiana turned to leave.

"I am sorry for raising my voice at you, cousin," Thomas said. "But I hope you will take my advice."

The sound of her footsteps was his only reply.

CHAPTER 23

Sixteen Years Earlier

The young maid held the infant in her arms, rocking him slowly while humming a soft lullaby. The baby was asleep. His head rested in the maid's arms, his body swaddled in the newly knitted blanket.

The baby's dark head of hair was charming, along with his full cheeks and bright eyes. He favored Lord Hopkins. Betsy paced the room, aware that the babe was beginning to stir.

Lady Hopkins lay motionless. Her face was pale, and she had hardly eaten for days. She had only spent three days in recovering since the birth. The birth had been her most difficult yet, and the doctor was concerned with her amount of blood loss. He declared it would be catastrophic were she to have another child.

Lady Hopkins smiled briefly at Betsy, reaching her arm toward the baby. Betsy indulged her, carefully placing little Phillip John beside her. Betsy faltered slightly at the weight of the babe in her left arm.

"And what a strong boy he will be, ma'am." She laughed, misty in adoration. "Little Phillip will be a good master, just as his papa."

Lady Hopkins did not meet her gaze. She traced the small baby's features with her finger, resting it over his chest. She closed her eyes. At last, she exhaled and offered, "John. We shall call him by his second name, John."

There was no use arguing with such an ill woman, and so Betsy only nodded, picking up her soft lullaby once more. Surely the mistress would come to see the child must be called after his father. Lord Hopkins had wanted a son for so long, and the doctor had made it painfully clear that Lady Hopkins was not to have another. Yet, Betsy could not help her recollections. Lady Hopkins and Lord Hopkins had not seemed happy for the past three years that Betsy had worked for them. Betsy thumbed through the folded linens on the dresser. She forbade herself to think the unthinkable, but still it came. Perhaps Lady Hopkins did not want to call the babe after his father because she did not wish the son to become as Lord Hopkins.

CHAPTER 24

Sixteen Years Later

Caroline and Lucy spent the morning strolling the cobblestone street, stopping every so often to glance at the smallest of trifles. Lady Hopkins had sent the girls off for a day of shopping, in what Caroline could only guess was an attempt at restoring Lucy's spirits before the spring ball. The sisters had spent the last hour looking at ribbons, gloves, and bonnets. At the moment, Caroline found herself on a street merchant corner. Lucy was enthralled with a small brooch. It was a curious, outlandish thing, carved from ebony into the shape of a rose blossom, the tips of the petals frosted with a delicate ivory paint.

"All the way from Africa?" Lucy asked the merchant.

It was clear to Caroline that Lucy had no desire for the brooch, but rather was interested in its origin only. Caroline distracted herself by glancing at a crate of imported silks. She found a soft pink shade that she found to her liking. It was absurdly priced, but still she held the fabric toward the sun, examining it as the light sparkled through the fibers.

"Mr. Clark! How wonderful to see you again," Caroline heard Lucy say.

Caroline's eyes shot upward as she lowered the fabric sheepishly.

Mr. Clark stood several feet off, chatting openly with Lucy. Caroline felt her face color as the man turned toward her and smiled. She took a step toward Lucy, absentmindedly dropping the pink silk to the ground. Mr. Clark bent down, and the two almost collided as he retrieved the small pink pile.

Caroline sighed as she straightened her stooped back. "Mr.

Clark, I seem to have had another stumble. I am beginning to grow accustomed to your rescue." She smiled at him genuinely.

His dark eyes searched her expression with a hint of sadness. "I am happy to oblige you, Miss Hopkins." He stood, folding the silk into a presentable bundle.

Caroline looked to Lucy. Her sister was busy purchasing a handful of trinkets now. "My sister and I have been on an errand to retrieve a few additions for our attire this evening. We are to attend the spring ball. Will you be there? It is supposed to be quite the party."

Mr. Clark shrugged his broad shoulders, leaning from his left to right foot. "Not if I can help it. Georgiana is always so insistent. She has put my name on the list, though I doubt I shall make it."

Caroline's countenance fell. She forced her mouth into a charming smile as she prodded the man. "I have heard a great deal about your dancing, Mr. Clark. I would consider it a shame if I did not have the chance to see you at your finest."

Mr. Clark unexpectedly laughed. "Are you encouraging me to attend for your sake?"

Caroline only smiled, tilting her head. "Perhaps, but it might do you some good as well."

Mr. Clark stared back at her with a small grin.

"Until tonight then, Mr. Clark?" Caroline boldly asked.

Lucy was making her way to the pair of them, a small package clutched to her side.

Mr. Clark peered around the street corner. "Perhaps I shall attend, if nothing more than to show you the proper way to dance."

Caroline's eyes sparkled at this, a mischievous grin stretching across her feminine features. "Of course. I shall save you the third dance."

"Good day, Miss Hopkins," Mr. Clark said with a bow.

"Good day," Caroline called back.

After a few strides, Caroline turned back to see Mr. Clark standing at the merchant's square alone, the pink silk still tucked in his ungloved hand.

CHAPTER 25

Lucy and Caroline stood to the side of the great room, awaiting the start of the ball. Lucy had dressed in a pale pink gown with exquisite lacing near the bodice and short sleeves. Her brown hair hung elegantly around her face, twisted into an elaborate maze of curls on her head. The pink blossoms, sent to her earlier from Mr. Frandsen, were situated between the curls beautifully.

Caroline stood in stark contrast to her sister's feminine choice of color. The bold emerald green of Caroline's dress caught the eye of almost all who passed. The elegant way in which Louisa had managed Caroline's hair was a drastic change from the usual twists and pins.

"How do I look, Caroline?" Lucy whispered in Caroline's ear.

"Oh, Lucy. You look stunning. I think Mr. Frandsen will have difficulty conversing with such an angel."

Lucy blushed at Caroline's words, bringing her gloved hand to her chest. "You must not tease me so." Then, in what Caroline could only guess was the result of an amusing thought, Lucy smiled. She leaned toward Caroline and said, "But to be fair, I think Mr. Clark will have to reconsider dancing only once with you!"

Caroline pursed her small lips together furiously, attempting to conceal her surprise. "I hear he is a fine dancer," she said flatly.

"So you said, earlier," Lucy mused.

Caroline found herself blushing. Thankfully, the ball began, and Caroline was whisked away by Mr. Low, whom she had met in town the previous week. He had begged for the first two dances, of which Caroline had agreed to happily. Mr. Low kept good conversation, though Caroline admitted to herself she was distracted. She had continually scanned the room for Mr. Clark for almost the entirety of the first dance. At long last, she spotted him dancing with Georgiana.

The second dance ended, and Mr. Low escorted her to the side. He thanked her. "Miss Hopkins, you must allow me to tell you what a fine dancer you are. I hope I shall have the opportunity to dance with you again," he said with a bow and turned in search of his next partner.

Caroline peered above the crowd for Mr. Clark when she felt a tap on her shoulder. She turned in surprise. "Mr. Clark, there you—" she started, until her eyes met the solemn face of Lord Searly.

His face, normally lit up with amusement, was cast down in a small pout. His eyes were searching, and his normally confident stance appeared stooped and shaky. The two had not spoken since their quarrel. After several seconds of uncomfortable silence, Lord Searly stepped forward. "Caroline, you look well this evening. Please say you'll dance with me."

Caroline smiled hesitantly. She felt bad about the offense she had caused him, but she did not want to miss her dance with Mr. Clark. "I have already engaged myself for this dance. Perhaps later?" She cocked her head to the side as she looked up at him.

His face fell, and he fidgeted with his hands. "I should have assumed as much. Your dance card must be full."

She saw the embarrassment written across his face. "You are mistaken," she said softly. "I have hardly spoken but two words to any gentleman tonight other than my last partner."

"Then you will dance with me?"

"Certainly."

Thomas watched the two conversing. The duke looked at Caroline with such hope and affection. It did not come as a surprise to Thomas, for he had heard the London gossip as every man did. Lord Searly had his heart set on Caroline. The thought of that arrogant man pining for Caroline brought an undeniable irritation once more. Thomas moved slowly toward the pair, unsure of what he should do.

"Ah, Mr. Clark!" Caroline spewed awkwardly when she saw him, "I was just looking for you."

Lord Searly looked annoyed at the interruption, clasping his hands behind his back as he lifted his head backward. "Ah, Mr. Clark, good to see you again."

Thomas nodded. "Always a pleasure, Your Grace. I am afraid I have disturbed your conversation."

Caroline waved a hand at him while shaking her head. "You did nothing of the sort. The duke has just promised me a dance later this evening. Isn't that right, Lord Searly?"

The duke bowed slightly. "Of course."

Thomas extended his arm toward Caroline, refusing to acknowledge to himself how beautiful she looked. He led her to the line of ladies in the center of the ballroom.

"I am glad to see you have come," Caroline said. "I worried I would be without a partner."

Thomas did not reply. He was certain she would have found a partner in Lord Searly.

"That is—I would not wish to be dancing with another partner. You cannot doubt my meaning."

Thomas wrinkled his nose and answered playfully. "Naturally, I believe you when you say you prefer my company to that of the duke."

They drifted apart as the dance progressed, exchanging with other couples and only stealing glances of one another at crossings. When at last they met near the center of the floor, Thomas was startled to hear Caroline laughing. He pulled her back to his side with a possessive curiosity.

"Why are you laughing?"

His question seemed to only spurn further laughter. The two were stepping toward a line in perfect harmony. Thomas's brows were furrowed as he waited for her response.

Caroline composed herself and finally offered, "I am pleasantly surprised, Mr. Clark. You dance beautifully."

Thomas shook his head. "No, there is something more. Out with it."

She bit her lip. "You suppose there is more meaning to my laughter? Perhaps I laughed because you never cease to surprise me. Whether it is saving me in the Jasper's parlor or dancing like a dandy—"

Mr. Clark held a finger up in protest and shook his head emphatically. "I do not dance like a dandy. I'll have you know that I learned in Paris."

Caroline's eyes threatened laughter once more. He had halted their promenade. He found his steps at last as he twirled her toward another partner. The two maintained eye contact as they weaved through one another. Thomas softened his gaze, and Caroline was smiling at him when the music ended. Their hands lingered in one another's as the crowd erupted in chatter.

Thomas's eyes darted across the dance floor to Lucy. He still had not decided what to do about Charles, but he knew that Georgiana had decided the task should fall to him.

With a startled movement, Thomas realized Caroline's hands were still in his own. He dropped them, offering his arm instead. "I apologize, Miss Hopkins. I am not quite myself tonight. I suppose you will call my cousin's bluff. You see now I am a distracted dancer."

"Are you quite all right?"

Thomas exhaled loudly. He did not want to distress her, and so he only shook his head dismissingly.

"I find you are a fine dancer, but perhaps you are in need of fresh air?"

The bright eyes that stared up at him weakened his resolve to forget his feelings. Caroline's hand now rested tenderly on his arm, and he found his defenses were useless. "You are right. Fresh air is just the thing to restore me."

As they walked toward the gardens, Thomas slowed his pace, though he felt his heart had done just the opposite. The evening air was crisp, and the moon shone brightly. The slight fog allowed the lanterns on the terrace to glow warmly.

The pair had grown quiet, though all around was filled with gaiety and clamor. Thomas did not want to leave Caroline's side, but his conscience filled with images of Lucy. He knew he must reveal the scheme soon. Lord Hopkins had not come to the ball, and Thomas struggled in deciding his course of action. He needed the help of someone with more influence than himself, though he could only think of one person, and the thought of asking *his* assistance aggravated Thomas. He would need to talk to Lord Searly.

Lord Searly watched in trepidation as Caroline hung on the arm of Mr. Clark. He was feeling increasingly nervous. He did not like to be at odds with Caroline. He was, of course, in love with her. But even more so, Lord Searly did not like seeing Caroline so at ease with another gentleman. She had not given him any promise; only the promise of contemplating his offer, yet Lord Searly felt responsible for her nonetheless. He would not stand to see her put him off so, and for a cordwainer no less. He did not detect a serious attachment on Mr. Clark's side, but Caroline's admiration for the man did not escape Lord Searly's notice. She had been flirting with Mr. Clark for the whole of the last dance. He had had enough, when he witnessed Mr. Clark's serious expression and penetrating gaze at Caroline. The duke started forward, only to be stopped by a strong arm that gripped his own.

"Jonathon!" Mr. Frandsen said. "It is good to see you, even if you were impervious to my attempts to get your attention." Lucy had Mr. Frandsen's other arm.

"David, it is good to see you!" Lord Searly said as he attempted to swallow his jealousy. "Miss Hopkins, will you allow me to tell you how pretty you look tonight?"

Lucy smiled, offering her hand to the duke, and before Lord Searly was aware, he was involved in a lengthy discussion with the two. His cousin had a way of drawing people in without their conscious consent.

"Are you always in town, Mr. Clark?" Caroline asked candidly.

"Why, yes, of course. That is—I have my work to attend to. I rarely find the time for travel—" He paused, shaking his head. "I suppose I could find the time to travel, but to be frank, I do not have a great many places to visit. I visit my parents, and my mother comes to London to stay with me every now and again. My brothers are in the navy, and I do see them when they do come to town on leave."

A slight breeze ran across Caroline's face, blowing a few stray curls across her cheek. She welcomed the cool relief as she sat in admiration of Mr. Clark. He was so sure of his place in the world, so at ease with his life. "I suppose you have lived a very different life than mine, but I hope it is not so different that we cannot be friends?" Caroline asked sincerely.

"Of course," he replied, but he was looking in the dark night distractedly.

"Will you call me Caroline then?"

Mr. Clark startled, placing both hands to his lapel in surprise. He turned to face her, only managing a coarse whisper. "If it would please you, of course. You must call me Thomas then."

Caroline smiled playfully. "I suppose I *must*."

Caroline thought she noticed Mr. Clark's dimple rise.

"Caroline, there you are!" Lord Searly exclaimed, grabbing her hand. He then turned toward Mr. Clark. "Mr. Clark, good evening! It must be a special treat for you to be in company with such beauty."

Caroline's blush rose, and she felt a sort of anger rising within her as well. She knew it was a compliment, but she felt the slight to Mr. Clark.

Mr. Clark, however, seemed to take no notice. Instead, he looked rather impatiently toward Lord Searly, "Your Grace, I must speak with you. It is of an urgent matter."

Lord Searly cocked his head backward as he laughed. Caroline cringed as the duke took Mr. Clark by a shoulder and pulled him aside. "Mr. Clark," Lord Searly said, leading him toward the ballroom, "You amuse me so. I cannot begin to imagine your urgency. I must tell you, though, I have an urgent matter to attend to myself. I owe that lovely lady a dance." He gestured toward Caroline and began striding back to her, unaware of Mr. Clark's hold on his arm.

It was then that Caroline could only see Mr. Clark whisper something to Lord Searly, which caused the duke to unexpectedly turn and follow Mr. Clark to the ballroom, leaving Caroline alone to ponder what was amiss.

Chapter 26

"You are sure of it, Clark? Your cousin is positive of the scheme?" Lord Searly was pacing anxiously.

Thomas was still, allowing himself a small reply. "I am certain."

"And where is she now—your cousin, Miss Georgiana? Did she not have the character to inform Lucy herself?" He stopped, the blood rising to his face. "Or did she wish to wait until it was too late, until Lucy was in fact trapped by that Jasper scoundrel?"

As if by magic, Georgiana appeared, gripping Thomas's side and staggering as she tried to catch her breath. "Tom, it's so much worse than I ever thought." Her eyes were filled with tears, her face pale.

"Georgiana, what is it?" Thomas asked, grasping her by her shoulders. "You must sit. Please excuse my cousin, Lord Searly."

Georgiana's eyes widened at seeing Lord Searly while in such a distressed state.

"Go on, Georgiana. The duke is here to help," Thomas explained.

Georgiana swallowed. "Tom, I had not thought Charles capable of such a plan. I only just heard him rehearsing the scheme with my aunt. They—" She turned to point, jumping slightly. "Oh, Tom. We must hurry. They are already about it!"

Lord Searly began nodding emphatically, if not somewhat haughtily. "Right you are, Miss Georgiana. Come, let us make a scheme of our own. We will not let this Jasper fellow dirty Lucy's reputation."

Mr. Clark nodded in agreement, but he sensed it was not Lucy's reputation Lord Searly was so concerned about.

Lucy had just finished the reel, when her leg suddenly cramped, sending a shooting pain down her foot. She let out a small moan, clinging tighter to Mr. Frandsen's arm.

"Miss Hopkins, are you hurt?" Mr. Frandsen asked, his eyes meeting her own.

Lucy smiled. "I am sure it is just a cramp. I suppose I could use a rest." She pointed to a soft chair not far from the ballroom entrance.

"Of course. You must sit. Allow me to fetch you some refreshment."

Lucy nodded, thankful. "That sounds like just the thing, Mr. Frandsen."

He left quickly, making his way through the crowd across the room, leaving Lucy alone to recover. Her leg felt stronger already, and she determined the cramp had been nothing more than the result of the dancing exertion. Lucy allowed herself to lean back in the soft chair and enjoy the cool mist from the nearby open door. She closed her eyes, pondering the pleasant night, specifically her time with Mr. Frandsen.

"Ah, Lucy, I am so pleased to see you enjoying a moment of reverie."

Lucy's eyes shot open, surprised at the sound of Mrs. Jasper's voice.

"Mrs. Jasper, I had not seen you. Please forgive me," Lucy said, straightening her gown.

Mrs. Jasper smiled, revealing her jagged teeth. "Oh, think nothing of it. We neighbors must always make special allowances for one another." She paused, hacking a loud cough into her handkerchief. "We have always, after all, been the greatest of friends, yes?"

Lucy nodded uncomfortably. "Why of course, Mrs. Jasper, the greatest of friends."

Mrs. Jasper began hacking again. "You must excuse me. The London air has never agreed with my disposition. I am afraid I should not have come tonight, especially without my Charles to accompany me."

"Charles is not with you?" Lucy asked, her brow furrowed. Mrs. Jasper seldom did anything without her son. In fact, Lucy could not even remember one time her neighbor had attended any public function without Charles.

Mrs. Jasper closed her eyes and shook her head spastically. "This is not the place for Charles. He would never fit in such a circle."

Lucy bit her lip, fearing her repulsion for Charles might betray her to the mother. "Then you are quite alone?"

Mrs. Jasper coughed once more. "Yes, my dear. Perhaps you would be so kind as to escort me to my carriage? I do not think I can manage the stairs without support."

Lucy glanced toward the ballroom. Mr. Frandsen was conversing with another gentleman. Lucy felt her spirits fall. "I would be happy to assist you," she lied, standing up and offering her small arm to the round woman.

"Oh, thank you. You have no idea the trouble I've been dealing with. I knew I could count on you to help," Mrs. Jasper said with a crooked smile.

Lucy only nodded, confused at the woman's forced politeness. Mrs. Jasper was never one to offer kind words unless there was something she wanted in return. Lucy hoped Mrs. Jasper's polite efforts were made only out of gratitude and not in an attempt to reconcile Lucy and Charles. It would never happen, Lucy determined. She would not ever speak to Charles Jasper again, if she could help it.

The odd pair made their way down the stone steps carefully. Lucy could not help her staring at Mrs. Jasper. The woman seemed to miraculously improve, not even stopping to cough once. Even more surprising was the fact that Mrs. Jasper seemed to lean on Lucy's arm less with each step. Lucy thought she saw the hint of a smile spread across Mrs. Jasper's pointed features as the two stepped toward the carriage. Lucy felt an uneasiness begin to rise in her chest. She glanced around the dark street nervously. Dark carriages lined the cobblestone street, and the only sound she heard was the quiet breathings of horses.

"Do you think you can manage from here, Mrs. Jasper?" Lucy asked, taking a step backward. "It is very cold tonight, and I seemed to have forgotten my cloak."

Mrs. Jasper clutched Lucy's arm tighter, pulling her forward quite forcefully. "Just a few steps more, darling girl."

Lucy felt her pulse quicken and her mind race, and she saw the outline of a dark figure emerge from the opposite side of the steps. She dared not turn her head to look closer, fearing it might indeed be Charles. The street began spinning around in her head. *Run*, she commanded her body. *Run!* Yet, to her surprise, nothing happened. She could not even open her mouth to scream. Panic had set in, and before she knew it, Mrs. Jasper and Charles had lifted her into the carriage.

They rode in silence for some time. Lucy was wedged between the mother and son, each of them holding one of her arms tightly.

"Where are you taking me?" Lucy finally asked, shaking.

Mrs. Jasper pulled back the carriage flap, glancing out in the dark. "Not much farther," she mumbled to herself. Lucy waited for a more pointed reply, but found neither Charles nor his mother intended to address her, at least not yet.

As the carriage continued, Lucy was sure she was not near anything familiar. The odors of the street had become fouler, the lanterns dimmer. At last, Mrs. Jasper scratched her chin, an animated smile appearing. She raised her voice to the driver. "You may pull off here, Mr. Worsley. And if you would be so kind as to go for a small walk, we'd be much obliged. This should only take a few moments."

"Aye, my lady," the driver answered, dismounting the carriage.

Mrs. Jasper laughed to herself, as she moved across the carriage so she could face Lucy. "I must thank you for obliging me so. I have arranged this meeting so that you might reconsider your answer to my dear Charles. Charles?" She said, turning to the son.

Lucy had not heard a word from Charles. Now that the carriage had stopped, his grip on her arm had loosened, and he allowed Lucy to scoot a few inches away from his side. She dared to look up at him.

Charles was swallowing breaths at an alarming rate, his face redder than Lucy had ever seen it. Unlike his mother, Charles lacked her excited posture and looked almost as frightened as Lucy.

"Yes, Charles, what do you have to say to me?" Lucy asked impulsively, summoning all the courage she had. She would not allow him the ease of having his mother answer for everything. If Lucy was going to be ruined, she wanted Charles to admit his part in it.

At the sound of her voice, Charles seemed to soften. His face fell, and he let out a small sigh. "Miss Lucy, I do not want to hurt you. Please spare you and me the pain. Accept my proposal, and be my wife." His voice was even higher pitched than normal.

Lucy gritted her teeth. "And what will you do if I refuse?"

Charles looked toward his mother.

Mrs. Jasper clapped her hands together, squealing. She pointed out the window at the small and dirty structure. "You see, my dear, we are at the entrance of a most despicable inn. We only have to check you and Charles in for the night. I have it on good authority that this is the inn that all the gentlemen of rank go when they do not wish to be discovered. But then again, no lady of any standing would ever be caught dead in such a place. And with a young man, unaccompanied? And for the whole of the night?" Mrs. Jasper's eyes widened as she shook her head reproachfully. "The idea! It is quite enough to ruin a duchess, let alone the daughter of a simple baron."

Lucy's eyes began to fill with tears. Never had she thought the Jaspers, her own neighbors, capable of such cruelty and shamefulness.

Charles turned and without looking down at her, asked more firmly, "Well, Lucy? Will you have me?"

Lucy shook her head to herself, clasping her hands together. "It sounds as if I have no choice, Mr. Jasper."

Mrs. Jasper began laughing hysterically. "That is the point, yes, but we must hear it from your lips."

The idea of being scandalized was so horrific for Lucy for she had always cared so much what others thought of her. She knew such a turn of events would ruin her chances entirely of making a good match, but the idea of marrying Charles Jasper did not seem any more promising.

A sudden tap at the carriage door interrupted Lucy's thoughts. Mrs. Jasper held her arms out, commanding Lucy and Charles to stay silent. Mrs. Jasper peeked out the carriage flap.

The old woman giggled softly. "'Tis only the driver." She opened the door a crack. "We are almost finished, sir. If you would be so good as to give us just a few more minutes—"

"I think not," the driver said, pulling back the door and removing his hat.

To Lucy's surprise, there stood Lord Searly with Mr. Clark a step behind.

Lucy shook as the tears poured out. "Lord Searly! Mr. Clark!" She flung herself toward the duke. "But how did you—?"

Lord Searly caught her in his arms, pulling her out of the carriage and handing her off to Mr. Clark. Mr. Clark grasped her shaking hand, pulling it into his arm.

"Never mind all that, Lucy," Lord Searly said, still staring into the carriage. "We can address that some other time. At present, I want to speak to *these* people." He paused, waiting for a response from Charles or Mrs. Jasper.

Lucy watched in horror as Mrs. Jasper perked up, offering a small giggle. "My lord, there seems to be some mistake."

Charles dabbed at his forehead. "Yes, of course, Your Grace, nothing amiss here." He laughed, though his voice shook and his face began sweating even more profusely.

"Is that so?" Lord Searly asked the pair, tapping his finger against his chin. "For Mr. Clark and I heard much darker threats than what is customary for a friendly reunion. Tell me, Mr. Clark, do you often hear young ladies being threatened with ruin if they do not accept a proposal of marriage?"

Lucy looked up at Mr. Clark, her hand still in his arm. He shook his head and answered in a deep voice. "Certainly not, Lord Searly."

Mrs. Jasper began laughing hysterically. She swatted a hand at Lord Searly's lapel. "Oh, dear," she said, breathing heavily between laughs. "It seems you have it all wrong, my dear duke." She grabbed at her side, as if the laughing was causing her pain. "What a joke we have played!"

Lord Searly's expression remained serious.

"Oh come, Your Grace. You must see the humor in all this," Mrs. Jasper was saying, her face reddening more with each moment that passed. The woman was clasping her hands together so tightly that Lucy could see some of her fingers turning a deep shade of purple.

Mr. Clark cleared his throat loudly.

Lord Searly turned and nodded at Mr. Clark. He looked back to the Jaspers. "Enough," he hissed. "It does not take much to see what you are after; you are a scheming woman and your son is reprehensible. Miss Lucy would have been better off ruined than forged with the likes of Charles Jasper and his mother."

Mrs. Jasper and Charles fell silent. Lucy had never seen Mrs. Jasper looking so ill. The distress upon being discovered had caused the woman to sweat at her hairline, sending small frizzed curls in a fan around the old woman's face. Her powder and blush were now running down the sides of her cheeks, and her raspy cough had returned.

Charles looked no better. His shoulders were hunched over his belly, his face sunk into his chest. His hair was completely soaked, and slobbery drool pooled down one side of his chin. For once his face was pale, instead of its usual shade of red, and his protruding teeth rested on his bottom lip, completely covering it.

Lord Searly sighed. "With Mr. Clark and myself as witnesses, the pair of you should be sent off to the gallows for kidnapping this woman." He stopped, shaking his head and stretching his arms out. "But I might be inclined to keep silent about this whole affair, if—"

"If what, my lord?" Mrs. Jasper asked in a desperate tone. Lucy was glad to see the old woman honest at last.

"If you never come near this young lady or her family again. Mr. Clark and I will, of course, take precautions. We will each make written statements that will be collected by my lawyers and put away for safekeeping. If I hear a word about you harassing this family again, or if I see you, *you* will be ruined, my *dear* Mrs. Jasper. Every column of every paper will declare your misdeeds. I swear it." He took a deep breath, and with the hint of a smile, he added, "And as a word of caution, do not ever get into a carriage without checking your driver. Fortunately, I had your Mr. Worsley follow in my carriage. He will now escort you home in yours."

With that, Lucy watched as Lord Searly slammed the carriage door shut.

When Caroline had received the note to return home immediately, she had not expected to find Lord Searly and Mr. Clark in the sitting room with her mother, father, and Lucy. By the looks of things, Lord Searly and Mr. Clark had only just arrived. Mr. Clark's nose was still pink from the cold, and Lord Searly was rubbing his hands together, as if to rub out the chill. Caroline immediately detected a look of alarm on everyone's faces.

"I came as quickly as I could. What happened?" Caroline asked, looking from face to face.

Lucy's shoulders caved as she ran toward Caroline. "Oh, it was absolutely horrible, Caroline! If it wasn't for Lord Searly and Mr. Clark, I am afraid I would be ruined!" She was speaking much too quickly and she had to stop to catch her breath.

Lady Hopkins stood from her chair, shaking her head. "Mrs. Jasper, our neighbor and friend of so many years, lured Lucy into her carriage by taking advantage of her sympathy, only to threaten her with ruin if she did not accept Charles's offer of marriage."

Caroline startled, clutching her sister's hand tightly. "You are not serious?" she asked, though she could see the answer in each of the faces staring back at her.

Lady Hopkins's eyes were filled with tears. "Oh, Caroline, nothing could be more true. If it wasn't for the way in which Lord Searly," she paused, turned, and reached for the duke's hand, "intervened, I am afraid our Lucy would have either been ruined or forced to endure the most horrific of marriages imaginable."

Lord Searly shook his head. "Your mother exaggerates my role, Caroline."

Lucy's hand flew to her chest. "She most certainly does nothing of the sort, Lord Searly! Why, to see the way you spoke to them, put them in their place." She turned to Caroline. "He was brilliant. He came to my rescue just as I was beginning to lose all hope."

Lord Searly's eyes were fixed on Caroline, and she could not help but feel the whole room was watching the pair. He smiled, pulling back his shoulders. "I admit my involvement, though I must not take all the credit. Mr. Clark was the one to first inform me of the scheme."

Caroline turned her head toward Mr. Clark, who stood seemingly forgotten behind Lord Hopkins. "Is it true, Mr. Clark?"

Mr. Clark shrugged. "I am only grateful Miss Hopkins has been spared such humiliation."

Lord Hopkins nodded. "Yes, as we are all, Mr. Clark. I cannot tell you both how indebted we are to you. The thought of the Jaspers threatening my girl . . ." Caroline's father's face was red, as he shook his head back and forth. His fists were clenched, and Caroline saw he was struggling to maintain his composure. Lord Hopkins was seldom angry and certainly not like this.

Lucy's shoulders began to tremble as she let out a small cough.

Caroline looked at her sister in concern. Her mother must have sensed Lucy's affected state as well for Lady Hopkins announced, "Gentlemen, we are most grateful, but I am afraid I must retire and care for Lucy. She has been through quite the ordeal tonight."

Lucy did not protest in the least, caving into her mother's outstretched arm. Together they left, Lucy bursting to tears as they reached the stairs.

Mr. Clark was the next to leave, offering a small bow to Caroline. Lord Hopkins escorted him to the door, leaving Caroline alone to face the duke.

Caroline took a seat on the sofa, her hands running across the soft velvet fabric. She had not been able to meet Lord Searly's eyes for a while, sensing his ardent and penetrating glances at her. She fidgeted with the fringe on one of the throw pillows. "Lord Searly, you must know how grateful I am for the service you have provided my family, and especially, Lucy. I could not bear to see her so unhappy."

The duke came to her side, knelt beside her, and grasped her hand. He stared up into her eyes. Caroline blushed, her eyes darting back to the pillow in her hand.

"You must know I did it for you, Caroline. Of course I care for your sister's happiness, but it was with you in mind that I intervened without a second thought." Lord Searly tugged at her hand as if to gain her gaze once more. Caroline nervously glanced back at him. "Please tell me you are still considering my offer?"

Caroline slowly pulled her hand back to her lap and smiled softly. "Of course I am considering your offer, Lord Searly."

Thomas stood in front of the window, glancing at the pair. He felt as if he did not even exist, watching as Lord Searly knelt beside Caroline. Thomas leaned against the street lamp, shaking his head wearily at what was inevitably to come. He contemplated how long it would be until he heard of the engagement between Lord Searly and Caroline, especially after the events of the night. It seemed certain to him now, but try as he might, he could not escape a sinking, miserable feeling.

CHAPTER 27

Ten Years Earlier

Six-year-old John was sitting on his father's lap. His face was soiled from playing in the gardens, and his newly pressed white shirt had streaks of mud across the front, but the boy seemed determined to learn to fold his father's cravat. Lord Hopkins had spent the last hour in amusement as he attempted to teach his son the gentlemanly art. He laughed out loud at John's most recent attempt.

"My little sir, you have done it all wrong! I shall never be admitted to tea in such a condition. Are you trying to discourage my chances of gaining your mother's favor, Johnny?"

John smiled at his father, revealing a small tooth that wiggled against his tongue.

"I suppose you are growing up. We must call you Lord John soon."

Lady Hopkins entered the library, carrying a book of accounts. She tossed the book down, her hands flying to her hips. "Phillip, your cravat is monstrous. Tea is in a quarter of an hour. And, I will not have you coddling the boy. I thought you knew my feelings on the matter. He is to be the heir, and he must learn as early as possible the truth of his responsibilities. John, come, let's get you cleaned up."

John obediently followed his mother, offering an attempted wink at his father. Lord Hopkins pressed a finger to his lips, his eyes shining with pride. He then opened the account book in front of him. The accounts had just been balanced, and he found he smeared a few of the newly inked numbers in finding the recent page. His accountant had been at work, and as was customary, Lady Hopkins had looked everything over prior to him.

Lord Hopkins offered a low grunt. His wife had never forgiven him. Though infinitely more aggravating to him was the fact that she had never forgiven him for something he had not been guilty of. Perhaps it had been so in the beginning, but in the end, he had married Eleanor because he loved her. And what was worse, despite his best efforts, she maintained the chip on her shoulder. Lady Hopkins refused to see her husband as a man desperately in love with her. She dismissed his compliments, shook away his advances, and seemed oblivious to his admiring glances. Lady Hopkins seemed to see only what she believed.

CHAPTER 28

Ten Years Later

"Lucy, you do not know your own mind, dear. I am sure you will regret it. Please trust your mother. I have seen so much more of life. I do not think Mr. Frandsen the match for you."

Lady Hopkins had been frantic all morning since she had heard of Mr. Frandsen's offer. He had spoken to Lord Hopkins who had happily given his consent, but Lady Hopkins demanded some time before hastily agreeing to such a match. Lucy had sat, seemingly unmoved by her mother's words of warning.

"You were not always this stubborn, my darling. Why, I remember just last season, you allowed me to talk reason to you about Mr. Jenkins's offer."

Lucy stood abruptly and moved near the window. "But I did not care for Mr. Jenkins."

Lady Hopkins trembled. "You have wounded me, Lucy."

The words made their mark upon Lucy, and her chest began to heave spastically as tears rushed down her pale face. "Mama, it is not that I am trying to be difficult. I would not dream of acting against your words if it was merely a matter of pride." She slowly turned, and as the tears continued to cascade down her cheeks, she fell into the arms of Lady Hopkins. "Mama, I love him. I do not wish to hurt you, only to secure my own happiness. Can you not trust my judgment?"

Lady Hopkins softened at this, but however touching Lucy's words were, Lady Hopkins still felt the need to shield her daughter from the repercussions of such a hasty decision.

"Are you quite sure Mr. Frandsen loves you?" Lady Hopkins cupped Lucy's face with her hands. "I do not wish to cause you pain, but are you quite certain it is you he loves and not your fortune?"

Lucy smiled at this. "Oh, Mama. I have never been treated with so much kindness and attention. Mr. Frandsen is incapable of trickery. He is the most honest man I have ever known."

Lady Hopkins sighed softly.

"I do not think a man could love me more," Lucy said, staring at her mother. Lucy's eyes seemed to sparkle as she described Mr. Frandsen to her mother. "He is so thoughtful, always looking after my comfort. I am sure he will make the most respectable and kind husband."

Lady Hopkins was silent for some time. At last, she cleared her throat resolutely. "I suppose his connection to Lord Searly is fortunate indeed. He does come from a good family, and I trust he treats you as you say. If these are your true feelings on the matter, I do not think I can dissuade you from your decision to accept his offer."

Lucy jumped in her seat at this, hugging her mother tightly as she cried with joy. She held her until Lady Hopkins could scarcely breathe. "Oh, thank you, Mama, for understanding. It would have broken my heart if you did not. You will see that David is superior to any other man I might have chosen.

Lady Hopkins smiled in relief. She had always had greater ambition for Lucy, but Lady Hopkins would not have her daughter be unhappy simply to please her. At least one thought eased her mind on the matter: Caroline would have an advantageous match.

The dinner party celebrating Lucy and Mr. Frandsen's engagement was quite the event. Caroline had never seen such a celebration. Lord Searly had insisted on hosting the party at his town home, and as was his style, the duke had made every detail imaginable something spectacular. The dinner itself had been excellent, prepared by the finest cooks in London. The meal had begun with a white soup, and had continued to include at least twenty different dishes, including fish, mutton, beef, pickles, an assortment of vegetables, puddings, jellies, cheeses, fruit, and nuts. Everything had been prepared to perfection, which came as no surprise to Caroline.

After dinner was served, the party retreated into the large music room. This room extended the length of the grand house and was filled with intricate tapestries, multiple seating areas, two fireplaces, a large piano, and portraits that stretched the entirety of the wall. On one side of the room were two separate doorways, each leading to a balcony that was lined with intricate sculptures and railings.

Caroline was seated by Lucy and Mr. Frandsen when Lord Searly came to her side. His shoulders were relaxed, and for once, the duke seemed to be without pretense. Caroline caught him staring at her.

"Lord Searly, please sit with us," Caroline insisted. "I was just telling Lucy and Mr. Frandsen how happy I am for them. Have you ever met two people better suited?"

Lord Searly sat by Caroline, glancing at Lucy and his cousin. "I must admit neither one of them could have found a more amiable companion. Once again, David, you must accept my sincere congratulations."

Mr. Frandsen smiled, grasping Lucy's hand. "I thank you, and I admit that for once, *you* are right."

Lord Searly grinned, leaning back against the elegant sofa. "I suppose I am right, though I never said you were the *most* suited. I know of one lady and gentleman that are of even superior compatibility."

Mr. Frandsen shook his head, leaning toward the duke daringly. His brows were furrowed, but Caroline sensed the corner of Mr. Frandsen's mouth threaten laughter. "And whom, may I ask, are you referring to?"

Lord Searly scratched his head, turning toward Caroline. "I suppose it would do me no good to tell you the answer to that question for I do not wish to upset the lady, though in time I hope you will see the answer yourself."

Caroline felt her face color, as she shook her head reproachfully. Lucy giggled.

Lord Searly smiled, seemingly pleased. He held his arm out to Caroline. "Will you take a turn with me?"

She wanted to refuse him after such a display. She crossed her arms and pulled her jaw forward, but when she saw the way Lord Searly's eyes rested on her own, she felt her heart quicken, and without another thought, she took his outstretched arm.

After only a few steps, Lord Searly began to laugh. "I thought you were about to refuse me."

"Perhaps I should have after your shameless talk."

Lord Searly nodded, raising one brow. "Caroline, you must know, you are proving my point quite conclusively."

"And what point is that?" she asked seriously, locking eyes with him once more.

"That we are best suited, of course! I cannot imagine a more fitting response to my outrageous ramblings. Only you are equipped to put me in my place. Other ladies would be too easily persuaded, but you—you would never dream of being controlled, not even in the slightest." The duke was talking softly, and Caroline recognized the affection in his tone.

"I suppose you mean it as a compliment, then?" Caroline asked, smiling.

"Can you doubt it?" Lord Searly asked, frowning down on her.

Caroline's shoulders began to shake as she laughed. "No, but most would not consider my stubbornness and independence as something to be admired."

Lord Searly tilted his head, shrugging slightly. They continued walking around the room, until they reached the piano. Caroline sat in a soft chair, watching as Lord Searly leaned against the wall. He was glancing at Lucy and Mr. Frandsen.

"They look so happy," Caroline remarked. "If it were not for you, we would not be celebrating this happy occasion."

Lord Searly pressed his lips together tightly, brushing his hair to the side. "Indeed. Not only would the happiness of my cousin and your sister have been prevented, but I suppose the pair of us would have had to suffer the connection to the Jaspers as well. Caroline, can you imagine what people would have said? Lucy and Charles, Lord and Lady Searly?" He stopped to shake his head, crossing his arms. "The thought of us being so connected! No, it would not do. Thank goodness the Jaspers' scheme was prevented." He looked at Caroline seriously, a small gleam dancing across his eyes.

Caroline smiled back, but quietly gasped at the realization of Lord Searly's much too obvious self-interest and presumption of their marriage.

CHAPTER 29

A ride in the park was just what Caroline needed to clear her head. The last two weeks had been nothing short of shocking and confusing. The Jaspers' wretched plan to force Lucy into choosing between ruin and marriage to Charles had indeed been upsetting. But Lucy had been spared. Lord Searly and Mr. Clark had come to Lucy's aid in what Caroline could only classify as providential. She was indebted to the gentlemen. From what Lucy had told Caroline, Lord Searly had played the largest role in the rescue and subsequent banishment of the Jaspers. This fact should have endeared the duke to Caroline more, and it had, but now Caroline struggled to know if her serious consideration of Lord Searly had more to do with his character or if it was more the gratitude she felt toward him.

Lord Searly had turned out to be much more complex than Caroline had ever thought possible. He was at times charismatic and entertaining, and at other times impertinent and arrogant. He was selfish and senseless, yet romantic and even brave. Caroline had at first considered Lord Searly's involvement in Lucy's rescue as purely noble. And it had been noble. He had done what was needed at a critical moment. The duke had claimed his involvement was solely out of consideration for Caroline, but the engagement dinner had taught Caroline otherwise, and she saw that Lord Searly would never do anything completely selflessly.

Caroline had been careful not to give too much encouragement to Lord Searly. Yet, he had spoken as if it was inevitable. So that was it. He considered the marriage between him and Caroline final. He had not even asked her properly. Further, was he really so certain she would accept his offer? She cringed at the thought of such arrogance. Perhaps it was expected, and perhaps it would be absurd to reject such an opportunity of wealth and prestige. *The Duchess of Rembridge*. Caroline mulled the title over in her head; she found it difficult to imagine herself in such a position. She was not ignorant of the many privileges that accompanied such a title and fortune. She was certain Lord Searly had decided on the marriage, and yet *she* did not feel so decidedly about the subject herself.

The season had brought so many surprises for Caroline. Nothing of immense proportions had occurred, but Caroline found herself with new ideas and expectations for her own life that were so very different than what she had considered before. She had not thought it possible to attain the good opinion of a duke, but it had been forced upon her almost upon the first moment of their meeting in Mr. Clark's shop.

Mr. Clark.

Caroline had tried not to think of him too often, but her feelings for him had transformed at an alarming rate. What once was mere intrigue had turned to attraction and pleasure, and now . . . Caroline hesitated to admit that she admired the man. She found herself reflecting upon him often. First, there was the matter of his looks. She found his dark features and strong jaw unmatched, the way his dimple appeared when he spoke or smiled simply charming. Then there was the way he spoke to her, the way he treated her.

Caroline envied Mr. Clark's determination and persistence. He had not been born into much, but he had traveled his own road to respectability. Caroline had frequently considered their respective stations. Lady Hopkins would never approve of such a match. She would tell Caroline repeatedly that she was meant for something greater, something more ambitious. Caroline herself acknowledged the inequality of such a match. Though, she felt she was sure it was quite the opposite. She would never measure up to such a man.

Caroline knew her own feelings, but Mr. Clark was guarded. She could not detect the degree of his affections. At times she was sure he considered her only a friend. Then there were moments when she felt his guard was down, when she saw him truly smile at her. When she had been recovering from her concussion, for instance, he had come to check on her. She felt sure he had been concerned, that he cared at least a little. She had shamelessly flirted with him at times, and she recollected how he had teased her back.

"Miss Caroline?"

Caroline turned to her groom, to see his face white in worry.

"We must turn back. The clouds threaten a spring storm and we are quite ill equipped for such a turn of events. Your mother would never forgive me if you were to catch a cold."

Caroline sighed. Such precautions. Caroline wished there were not so many limitations on women. A woman must never ride alone. A woman must never ride in rain, or wind, or anything exciting. A woman must always submit to every regulation of propriety. Caroline felt an impulse building inside. She watched as her groom trotted back to the path, heading for home. She spied a dark patch of trees in the distance. She turned slowly.

"George, will you allow me just a small pleasure?"

He nodded.

"Will you return home and reassure Mama I will be there soon? I simply wish to take a ride as if I was home, at Whitefield Hall."

George shook his head vigorously. He held his finger up as if in command. "Miss Caroline, I will not do anything of the like. You, a lady, riding alone! I would be shirking my duties if I ever saw it."

Caroline pulled her horse to a halt, pleading with all her might, "Oh, please, George. It is not so very unforgiveable as one is told. I am a lady after all—greater allowances are always given to those with the right reputation. Besides, I do not think I shall see above two people I may know today, the weather as it is."

George swallowed hard. Caroline knew she had always been his favorite. As a child, she had preferred to run along his side in the garden and stables than to sit with the women indoors.

"I cannot permit it." He grunted as he said it.

Caroline's countenance fell as she remained in step with him. With a sudden stir in the horse, she found her courage once more. "Then, by all means, do nothing of the sort!" she chimed teasingly as she broke to a sprint, leaving poor George neatly saddled as he shook his head disapprovingly. She did not worry at him following her. She knew he did not have the heart to reproach her, and she felt certain that though he may worry, she would not be deprived of her freedom.

Caroline's throat burned as she hurdled different obstacles, keeping her mare at a fair sprint. After what felt like an eternity, she slowed her horse to a stop near a stream. She dismounted, leaning against the horse's neck to rest.

"There, girl, drink," she commanded. The horse impatiently lapped the water, feeding on a few blades of grass. Caroline held to the reins as she walked along the stream in contentment. She found herself quite lost in the beauty and in the privacy she had found. She tied the horse and found the perfect spot to relax under a large oak tree.

She had only meant to lie for a moment, when her eyes closed, and she fell asleep.

She was awoken by the shakes of thunder. Caroline sat up, confused as to her surroundings. It was impossible to tell the time of day with the dark clouds. It was raining now, and Caroline furrowed her brows in dismay. How she had slept through rain escaped her. Although reluctant to leave her small freedom, she recognized it would be ill judgment indeed to stay longer. The storm was only just beginning. She attempted to mount the mare, but the horse startled at the clap of thunder. Caroline came down hard on her right foot, the heel of her riding boot breaking clean off the sole. She did not suppress the smile that came to her lips, as she at last mounted and broke into a gallop toward town.

"Caroline!" Lady Hopkins said reproachfully, rushing to Caroline's side. "How could you abandon your groom?"

Caroline was dripping from head to toe. She moved bashfully to the staircase.

Lady Hopkins did not fail to see her limp. "And have you injured yourself? Serves you right, you wretched girl."

Caroline smiled brightly, noting the concern in her mother's voice. "Oh, nothing of the sort, Mama. I was mounting that brown mare and came down hard on my boot. The heel has snapped clean off!"

Lady Hopkins shook her head disapprovingly once more. "You are lucky it was not your ankle."

"I will consider myself fortunate. It could have been worse. I suppose it will be of great comfort to you that I will not be able to ride again until this boot is repaired!"

Lady Hopkins smiled exasperatedly. "I shall count the blessing before me. Now, up to Louisa. She has a warm bath awaiting you."

Chapter 30

The next morning, Caroline set out to Mr. Clark's shop with her broken boot, along with Lucy and Louisa for company. The ladies found Mr. Clark detained for another twenty minutes, and Lucy begged Louisa to accompany her to Mrs. Privett's shop. Caroline promised she would join them directly. The two left hesitantly, with Lucy promising to search the dress shop for anything of interest to Caroline.

Mr. Clark's eyes widened when he saw Caroline. Caroline bit her lip, trying not to smile at his disheveled hair and the small flakes of wood that sprinkled it.

"Miss Hopkins, what can I do for you?" he asked, running his fingers through his hair.

"I hoped you could help me with a small repair on my riding boot."

He led her to a workstation in the back of his shop, and Caroline showed him the boot.

"A *small* repair? How ever did you manage this?" he asked, shaking his head.

Caroline looked down at her gloves as she started to explain. "Well, you see, Mr. Clark, I had a beautiful ride in the park yesterday. I took a small rest when it began to storm. I tried to mount the mare, but she was jittery. I came down hard on the heel. It snapped clean off."

Mr. Clark nodded, still inspecting the boot. "And where was your groom to help you?"

Caroline looked up at him, blushing. Her fingers twisted a small curl that had fallen at the nape of her neck. "I suppose I was rather awful and left the poor man."

Mr. Clark laughed loudly, dropping the boot to the table in front of him. He shook his head, staring deeply into Caroline's eyes. "You surprise me."

At that, Caroline stood a little taller. She paced along the edge of the table, inspecting all of the tools. "I hope I do." She paused, feeling her face start to color once more. "Are you able to repair it?"

He looked at her challengingly, "Of course I can. I will have it to you within a day or two at the most. The boot itself is still well intact."

Caroline gave a small laugh and added, "Of course. I did not mean to question your abilities. Thank you, Thomas." Her voice softened as she said his name.

Mr. Clark was fidgeting with the boot again. "And how is your sister? Has she recovered?"

Caroline's eyes fell. "She is much better. Thank you."

Mr. Clark turned toward her, his eyes filled with a look of concern. "I am glad to hear it."

Caroline took a step closer to Mr. Clark. "I have not yet thanked you for your role in preventing the scandal. It all happened so quickly, and I am still quite shocked by it all. How you came to play a part in the horrid affair has escaped me, but, I am indebted to you."

Mr. Clark shook his head. "I think Lord Searly would rather you were indebted to him."

Caroline heard the crack in his voice as he spoke and recognized the jealousy in his eyes. She smiled. Perhaps there was greater feeling behind his kindness. She stood to leave and impulsively took his arm. "Perhaps you are right," she said, "though I think if it were not for the service you rendered, Lord Searly would have been utterly useless."

Mr. Clark grasped her hand for just a moment, before the clerk entered and explained a customer had arrived in a frenzied state.

CHAPTER 31

Caroline followed Bentley to the small parlor to find Mr. Clark standing there stiffly. He was wearing his dark navy coat, the one she had seen him wear at Charles's party a few months ago.

"Mr. Clark, do you always dress so when you make your home deliveries?"

He nodded. "I do sometimes attempt to look like a gentleman."

Caroline did not laugh but instead examined his attire closely. "You look very smart."

Thomas shrugged and presented Caroline with her boot.

She examined his work, determined to find fault but found she could discover none. "Thank you, Thomas. I have been missing my rides. I find that none of my other boots will do. Although, after seeing your skill, I am determined to order a half dozen riding boots from you." She paused and smiled. "For who knows but that my poor boots take quite the beating from me."

Mr. Clark was now sitting beside her.

Caroline searched his face but found he did not seek her gaze. "I have the most pleasant of news! Can you guess it?"

He shook his head, his eyes slightly darkening. "I am afraid I have not the slightest idea."

Caroline laughed. "Mr. Frandsen has proposed to my sister Lucy, and she has accepted him! You cannot know the joy this brings to me to see such a sister, such a dear friend, happy. And to Mr. Frandsen! He is just the type of man to make Lucy happy."

Mr. Clark's eyes brightened. "I offer my full congratulations to you and to her. She deserves a life of happiness. I wish it were possible to congratulate her myself.

The room grew quiet, and the two sat for nearly a minute without speaking.

"Do you think you would enjoy matrimony?" Caroline asked. "Or are you determined to your bachelorhood like so many gentlemen of London?"

"I do not know," He said in a steady voice. "That is, I do desire to find a wife, but I know I cannot offer much to a lady."

"You are not impoverished, Mr. Clark. You are very respectable. I am sure you will provide sufficiently for such a lady."

He nodded, offering what looked like a sad smile. "You are kind, but I am afraid I cannot offer more than sufficiently."

"But is not character and love worth more than the distinction and luxuries you speak of?" Caroline continued, "Surely your qualities and company are offering enough!"

Mr. Clark's jaw came forward, and he sighed softly. He stared intently at her until she broke their gaze by standing and walking toward the window. He did not make a move toward her. "I am grateful you hold me in any sort of admiration, Caroline, but I cannot pretend your opinion is of the majority. I find myself in a difficult position. I deal with gentlemen and ladies of quality in my shop daily. Some consider me a gentleman as well, but I do not fool myself. A tradesman is still a tradesman. To think I could mingle in the same circles such as you is mere silliness."

Caroline turned toward him, the blood rising to her face, though this time out of anger. She shook her head as she sought for an appropriate response. "I am sure you do not mean that." The intensity of her tone and passion had risen. She closed her eyes and took a deep breath and continued. "It is, of course, more common for those of superior ranks to look down on tradesmen or the like and refuse such company, but for a man such as you to refuse your company to those of higher standing? You act as if you have nothing to offer them, or is there another reason?"

Mr. Clark stood at this. He placed both hands to his head in frustration. "It is nothing of the like. I have told you my exact reasons that I will never mingle in the London ton. What can it be to you, the lady that all of London knows will marry the Duke of Rembridge, the honorary Lord Searly?"

Caroline approached him timidly, curiously looking him up and down. "You do not think the duke a good match for me?"

Mr. Clark's eyes rolled backward in an irritated fashion. "On the contrary, he is the *perfect* match."

Caroline heard his sarcastic tone, and she nodded, urging him to continue.

"He is wealthy enough and from what I hear, quite handsome enough, though I only base that on the opinion of my silly cousin Georgiana. I had thought your character above his haughty and selfish ways. He would not appreciate you."

"No? Pray, continue, Thomas. What appreciation would he lack?"

His arms flew in the air as he approached the large window. He placed one arm above his head, leaning against the arch. "He does not deserve you."

Caroline smiled, though Mr. Clark did not see it, at last satisfied. She swallowed hard and found herself examining the newly repaired boot again. "I am sure you have many admirers. Perhaps if you were not *such* a gentleman, you would recognize there is at least one lady who holds you in affection."

Mr. Clark startled, almost losing his balance. Caroline noticed a small bead of perspiration slipping down the side of his cheek as he furrowed his brow. His face was drawn in an expression Caroline had never seen before. He looked in agony, and yet his eyes rested softly on hers. With a firm hand, he touched her cheek, and then carefully cupped her chin, kissing her lips softly and sweetly. The affection and attraction that Caroline had felt for months poured into the tender, albeit short-lived, kiss. A spilled pan down the kitchen hallway clamored across the house and awakened the pair to their surroundings. Mr. Clark instantly jerked backward, dropping his hands to his sides. They had not been discovered, but both knew they could not risk doing so again.

Caroline's tearful eyes were staring up at him longingly.

Mr. Clark's hand rested on his forehead as he staggered backward. "Caroline."

Caroline watched in confusion. She had caught the depressed tone of his voice.

He quickly took her by the hands, and whispered urgently, "It will not do." He then quietly rushed out the door, taking his leave.

Chapter 32

Lord Jonathon Searly had been the talk of the town for a handful of London seasons. Many even considered him the most eligible bachelor in all of England. The opportunities afforded to such a reputation had at first been enjoyable to him. He had enjoyed dancing with the prettiest partners and riding in the park with the most desirable friends. He had almost fancied himself in love four seasons ago to a Miss Anabelle Richmond. The girl had been beautiful and charming. She rode with him regularly in the park, even allowed him the most ridiculous of liberties. He had shared affectionate conversation with the girl. Miss Richmond had attached herself to him in every reasonable way the young girl could have—she laughed at his ridiculous jokes, she listened carefully to his political rambling, and even offered prolific conversation at times. He had been at the cusp of declaring himself to her, when he discovered a most unfortunate truth. Mrs. Richmond, a widow of nearly five years, had set her daughter's sight on Lord Searly long before the season had even begun. Through a very reliable source, the duke had been enlightened as to the extent of scheming and planning that had been involved with his first meeting with Miss Richmond.

Lord Searly had slighted Miss Richmond without a second thought. He boldly confronted her at a large concert gathering. Mrs. Richmond and her daughter had been thoroughly humiliated. The girl had attempted to explain herself in the most inappropriate and disgusting ways after that. She wrote him multiple letters for weeks, begging him to believe her. And then there was the mother, Mrs. Richmond. After the shameful spectacle, she had claimed to be on her sick bed for almost the rest of the season, something about the warm air inducing headaches.

Lord Searly was not deceived, though.

It had taken him some time to recover his senses. He had been in a depressed state and no longer attended public events or social gatherings. He spent his day sleeping, or worse, in the Prattler brothers' gaming house. It was only when his cousin David, then only nineteen, had happened upon his drunken state one morning.

David had been disgusted at the sight of him, being so bold as to slap Lord Searly across the face and exclaim, "Pull yourself together, Jonathon, for goodness' sake!" David had then thrown the bottle of port against the stone fireplace with great force, slamming the door as he left, leaving Lord Searly quite shocked.

After that, the duke had straightened his act, even finding the strength to entertain large crowds again and mingle in town. Though he played the incorrigible flirt, the truth of the matter was that Lord Searly had grown extremely bitter. He spent his days in enjoyment, but found he no longer trusted anything or anyone. This tactic proved a success, as nothing seemed to affect him again.

It was not until meeting Caroline that he had allowed himself to feel anything again. He did not even understand his fascination with the woman. Perhaps it was the fact that she did not try to attract him. Sometimes he even wondered if she was capable of caring for him. She seemed so distant, so lost in contemplation and thought. Try as he might, he could not win her easily. He found she was incapable of doing anything for ulterior motives. He loved her for it. If only he could make her see how happy they would be.

He was sure they would marry. Or *was* he? She was open with him, at times she even confided in him. He had enjoyed glimpses of her spirit and trust. Thoughts of her surprised expressions at his occasionally improper behavior left him smiling. He wanted nothing more. Yet, he was not so infatuated that he did not see the obstacles before him.

The most notable of such was Mr. Clark. Lord Searly had noted Caroline's frequent visits to his shop, the gossip of the Jaspers' house party, and the charming way in which the pair had danced at the spring ball. He knew there was no mistaking what he saw. He felt certain Mr. Clark, as honorable as he was, would not induce the girl to matrimony when such an advantageous alternative stood before Caroline. And what else could ensure her happiness more than rank and fortune? Lord Searly knew a passing fancy, and though he could never objectify Caroline as one, he knew Mr. Clark might come to see her as such someday. There was only one thing left to do, Lord Searly decided, and that was to notify Mr. Clark of his intentions with the girl.

The bell startled Thomas. He scarcely had time to straighten his attire before Lord Searly paraded in toward his drafting table. Thomas endeavored to conceal his contempt for the man. He knew there was no reason to resent the duke. In fact, he recognized Lord Searly's patronage as beyond fortuitous. It was the duke who first established Thomas's reputation of unmatched skill and craftsmanship in London. Yet, Thomas found his dislike for the man rising with every passing moment.

The two were conversing lightly, when Lord Searly's face darkened. He glanced over his shoulder and then began speaking in hushed tones. "Clark, my man, I cannot thank you enough. Your timely intervention has spared Lucy the most unfortunate of circumstances. Add to that the happy consequences of such gruesome events. My cousin David is now engaged to Lucy, and I am finally in favor with Caroline again. I owe you my profound gratitude. You must know that I am in your debt," Lord Searly explained as he placed his leg upon the stool that Thomas was sitting on.

His air of confidence and superiority had never seemed so exaggerated. Thomas continued carving his last. "I did not intend a favor in return. It was simply the right thing to do."

Lord Searly's laughter filled the shop, as he nodded amusedly. "Yes, you are quite right, Clark. It was the right thing to do. I see you think I am quite arrogant."

Thomas looked up from his work, staring blankly at Lord Searly in response.

"Yes, yes. I suppose I have been acting rather haughty. It is of no offense to you, Clark, for you see me as I am. I have been raised a duke, and remain a duke. I have not been taught the modesty you so naturally possess."

Thomas's jaw came forward as he clenched his teeth. He attempted at civility. "I have no reason to take offense from you. You are a loyal customer, and I am grateful for your business."

Lord Searly was clearly no longer listening. He now was focused on the sketch lying on the table. It was a sketch of a lady's leather riding boot, with intricate leather detailing.

"Extraordinary, Clark. Are these designs for a customer?"

Thomas shook his head. "It is just a project I have been working on in my spare time." They were, of course, sketches Thomas had made with Caroline in mind. Ever since Caroline's broken boot, Thomas was convinced she needed something more reliable.

Lord Searly was now holding the papers in his hand. "I simply must have you make these boots."

Thomas swallowed hard. "And what need have you of ladies' riding boots?"

Lord Searly laughed again. "Oh, I have a great need of them. I will give them to a certain lady as a bridal gift, when she accepts, you see. I have no doubt. You have Caroline's measurements, I presume?"

Thomas fought the urge to refuse, owing to his mounting workload. There was nothing that would be more infuriating than for Lord Searly to give the boots to Caroline. And yet, Thomas reminded himself that he would never be matched with her. She would, most likely, accept the duke's proposal. After a hard swallow and an inward groan, he nodded curtly. "I will get started right away, my lord."

"Wonderful, Clark. You must arrange the fittings and such. Until we meet again," Lord Searly responded pleasantly as he tipped his hat and let himself out of the shop.

Thomas muttered an incoherent farewell after the door slammed shut.

Joseph let out a loud "hmphff" but did not get up from his small desk.

Thomas exhaled loudly. "If you must say it, then say it."

Joseph remained silent.

Thomas, agitated as he was, found himself abandoning his work and striding around the curtain to face his clerk. "What? I see you have established an opinion of some sort. I can only guess it has to do with the duke."

Joseph straightened his posture; swiping his hand through his red and somewhat disheveled hair. "Come, Tom. Don't go making this about the duke. You know very well it's about you. You have feelings for Miss Caroline. Even I can see it, yet you allow *that* man to claim her as his bride without the slightest show of resistance. I thought you had more nerve."

Thomas's jaw was clenched again, his dark eyes full of stern indignation.

"Sir, if I may be so bold, I must say that you will live to regret it."

The words pierced Thomas. He shrugged, attempting to conceal his pain. He turned from his clerk and mumbled, "You imagine me severely affected by the girl, Joseph. Do not presume to give me advice."

Thomas was left in contemplation much of the day. The sky had turned dark, much like the expression on his face. Thomas had even sat at his drafting table for a full twenty minutes watching the rain beat against the window without the slightest sign of stopping. The streets began to clear until Thomas discovered it was pointless to keep the shop open. He dismissed his clerk early and set out at his drafting table to finish the day's work.

Thomas soon found, however, that his mind was much too preoccupied to get anything done. His thoughts had turned to Caroline. His mind reviewed the past months, stopping to illuminate on every detail of their meeting, the house party, her concussion, and the visits in the shop, until at last his mind rested on their solitary moment in her parlor but a week ago where they had shared a kiss. He had known nothing more appealing than the idea of a life with Caroline, but his sense of reality did not allow him to fool himself. Such a lady deserved more than he could offer.

Lady Hopkins had hardly sat a moment all day. With the preparations to leave town, the wedding shopping, and the persistent suspicion she felt about Caroline, her nerves had almost taken over entirely. Caroline had been acting strangely, and if Lady Hopkins did not know better, it looked as if the girl was heartbroken. Caroline had refused her morning tea, refused a ride in the park with Lord

Hopkins, and had been silently plucking at the piano all afternoon. Lady Hopkins had attempted at conversation, but her daughter had moodily left the room at the mention of Lord Searly. Lady Hopkins had only brought him up in a subtle, non-prodding sort of way, or so she thought. Her mothering instincts told her not to touch on the subject for the rest of the day. Perhaps something had happened between the pair to make Caroline so gloomy.

Caroline *was* heartbroken, though not for the reasons that her mother supposed. It had been over a week since her outrageous declaration to Mr. Clark. He had given her reason to believe he felt the same, but his stubborn resolution that "it would not do" had crushed her hopes and proved her fears. He had left her in a confused state, vulnerable from the emotions that always accompany a desired first kiss. She had waited to see if he would call on her in a few days, but he had not.

Caroline at first felt angry, but by late Saturday evening, she felt nothing but sadness. What was infuriating to Caroline, however, was her mother's awkward and tiresome attempts to "see what was the matter" with her. Caroline cringed at her leading questions, first about the latest social events and then her increasing specific questions about Lord Searly. Surely her mother should have seen that Caroline had much heavier ideas weighing on her mind.

On Monday morning Lady Hopkins instructed Caroline to look her nicest and be on her best behavior, as Lord Searly was to call on them. Caroline had obeyed mechanically, inwardly dreading the prospect of seeing the duke. Still feeling confused by her meeting with Mr. Clark, Caroline had been in no state to consider her feelings for another.

When Lord Searly had arrived, Lady Hopkins rose to the doorway before Caroline could even see the duke's face.

"My dear Lady Hopkins, how well you are looking."

Lady Hopkins smiled bashfully. "Lord Searly, you are too kind."

Caroline watched, unaffected, by the pair's idle chatter. First they talked about the weather, then the grand duchess, and finally, Lady Hopkins had turned the conversation to Lucy's wedding. It was not until Lord Searly glanced at his watch while tapping his foot softly that Lady Hopkins seemed to remember Caroline, who was seated beside her.

"You must excuse me, Lord Searly. As much as I enjoy our conversations, I suppose you have not come to chat with an old married woman." She smiled broadly, winking at the duke.

Lord Searly politely laughed. "Oh, but I do love our conversations." He cleared his throat, sitting a little taller. "But if I may, I would be most grateful for a moment to speak to Caroline alone."

"Of course," Lady Hopkins said, stroking Caroline's arm before leaving the small room.

Caroline startled at the sound of the latch, feeling a wave of anxiety rush over her. She sat nervously, fidgeting with the book beside her. She ignored Lord Searly's playful glance, and she made an attempt at seriousness. "I hope my mother has not taken too much of your time."

His smile faded as he moved closer. "I would not wish it any different, my love."

Surprised, Caroline's eyes darted to the floor.

"Have you had ample time to consider my offer of marriage?"

His question felt forced, and Caroline almost laughed aloud as she responded, "Oh, is that what it was? As I recall you never actually offered for my hand. You asked if you should talk to my father. I had not the least notion of your meaning more than political dealings or the like." She was teasing him, but only because of the bitterness she felt blossoming inside herself.

Lord Searly smiled. He did not seem to notice the hint of anger that lingered in her tone. "Caroline, you know what I am about. I want to marry you. Will you be my wife?"

Her heart began to beat faster. "I am indebted to you, Lord Searly, but I cannot give my consent as of yet."

He gave way to laughter. "I shall have to try again, yes?"

"Yes, some other day perhaps, when I am recovered from the shock of everything." She turned away from his intense scrutiny.

"And perhaps some days after that offer, yes? Or shall I be compelled to wait longer? Caroline, I am not the most patient of men."

The room felt smaller all at once, as if the walls were coming down on her. Caroline felt the heat rising in her chest as she shrugged her shoulders.

"Our marriage is expected, is it not?" He was kneeling beside her, as he ran his hands through his hair. His handsome gaze held hers, and he leaned toward her.

"I suppose it is, but expectations do not frighten me," she replied softly. "I cannot deny that I have considered it often. I feel indebted to you, Lord Searly." Her voice drifted as she realized the insufficiency of her feelings. "I have considered the possibilities as of late, but I am not convinced we would suit one another." She pushed herself off the chair, slinking away from his shocked and somewhat sick expression.

He stood anxiously and paced a moment, shaking his head in disbelief. His smile widened as he followed her across the room. "You cannot be serious, Caroline. I disagree wholeheartedly. I think we suit each other perfectly. You are the only woman in the world that would ever stand up to me. And, I suppose I am just the man for you, for who else would spoil you as I could? I would not get in the way of anything you desired. Can you not see my desire to please you? Do you not see the regard I hold for you? I regret I have not expressed myself well. I am not influenced by expectations or anything of the sort. Rather, I am compelled to offer for your hand because of the affection, even passion, I feel for you. I believe I have never loved another as I love you." His eyes were wide, and his confidence actually appeared to be shaken.

Caroline felt the weight of his words. For a brief moment, she considered accepting his offer. If she could not marry Mr. Clark, perhaps it did not matter if she married for love at all. If only she was convinced Lord Searly truly loved her, she knew she could will herself to love him back. Yet, there was something missing in it all.

Though Lord Searly professed love, Caroline did not believe it was, in fact, love. She exhaled quietly, finding her courage as she stepped forward to face him. "I admit it would do you good to have a wife that was not afraid to stand up to you, but you cannot think me equal to the task. I would tire of it." She paused, sensing his pain, and slowly started again. "I have been spoiled my whole life. It has not done me good. If we were to marry, can you not see the disaster we would become? I would work for nothing and gain even less. And, I promise, you would not be happy. You would tire of the arguing. I cannot imagine you would be happy."

Lord Searly jerked backward, almost losing his balance.

She realized she had caused him pain, but she could not deny the truth of her words. Caroline wondered if he had comprehended a word of her reply. She contemplated rewording it, when at last he broke the silence.

"I cannot compel you to marry me, Caroline. I suppose I thought it so because I wished it so. I have never been refused anything in my life." His shoulders stooped as he gave a soft chuckle. "Except for love. I chide myself now for thinking I could gain your favor. I should have known better." He attempted at playfulness, but Caroline heard the crack in his voice. His eyes were cast down, and his lips trembled.

Caroline grasped his arm in desperation. "Please, Lord Searly, you must understand. If I were convinced we could deal well together, I would not, in the least, utter a refusal that would cause you pain. But, as it is, I am convinced I shall not marry after all, or at least not for some time. My second season has been quite diverting and, somewhat exhausting, but I fear I have not yet found what I am looking for."

He listened, and for once, escaped his own self-pity long enough to clasp her hand in his. "I see we both have cast our eyes upon that which will never be ours."

Caroline froze, shocked by his perceptiveness. She opened her mouth to discredit him, but found herself stumbling over her words, and at last pulled her hand away, silently walking him to the foyer.

"Farewell, Caroline," Lord Searly said sadly. He took her hand and kissed it softly, bowing.

Caroline curtsied, surprised to find a tear rolling down her cheek. She felt the finality of her words. "Goodbye, Lord Searly."

The duke left determined to disguise his disappointment and confusion. For the second time, Lord Searly had been denied love. He fooled himself into believing he had been unlucky, that he had done everything possible to secure his own happiness. His contemplation was, however, short-lived. For after mere hours of his rejection, irritation replaced confusion. Anger overcame his sadness, and pride consumed his humiliation. The idea that he did not know how to love never entered his narrow mind. The unfortunate girl had given up her chance of becoming a duchess. He pitied her for he imagined she would live to regret her decision almost immediately. He would, however, not make the mistake of offering for Caroline, or anyone else like her, again. Perhaps providence had spared him twice.

Chapter 33

The excitement of Lucy's upcoming wedding had overwhelmed the house, especially Lord Hopkins. Lady Hopkins had determined she would return to Whitefield Hall within the month for preparations, for Lucy would be married at the parish in Chelmsford. Lady Hopkins had only to attend to the wedding clothes and other purchases in town before the family's departure. Lord Hopkins was pleased his wife now considered the match to be perfectly amiable. Mr. Frandsen was an agreeable sort of gentleman, and his success in attracting Lucy was the talk of the town. It was, of course, to be expected, for Lucy not only had a large fortune but was also beautiful and kind. Many said Lucy could have done better, but Lord Hopkins disagreed.

It was three weeks later that Lord and Lady Hopkins learned of Caroline's refusal to Lord Searly. Lord Hopkins had chuckled appreciatively on hearing the news, promising Caroline that *she* could do better. Lady Hopkins, on the other hand, had been in hysterics, declaring no man of consequence would desire a woman so conceited as to set her ambitions on a man of any higher standing than Lord Searly! Caroline had stood her ground, though solemnly, and dismissed her mother's raging comments and pleadings for her to reconsider her refusal. It could not be undone, however, and Caroline refused to say more on the subject.

It was in one of her more brooding moods that Lord Hopkins found his wife. He had been in the library searching for *The Discourse on True Horsemanship*, when he heard panicked sniffling. Lord Hopkins tiptoed his way toward the noise, at last discovering his wife sitting in the window seat. Her eyes were red from the crying, her nose pink. With one look at her husband, she threw herself across the seat, burying her head into a pillow.

"Eleanor, what on earth are you about?" He asked, confused. He sat beside her and gently stroked her hair.

Lady Hopkins pulled away from his touch. "I cannot stop thinking of what Caroline has done. She has thrown her future away, only to have the likes of fortune hunters and men of lesser means thrust upon her!" She buried her face in her hands, struggling to catch her breath.

Lord Hopkins observed his wife's frantic state. It seemed highly unwarranted. "You cannot be serious, my love. Caroline is quite capable of making an advantageous match. It is only her second season. She is not an old spinster yet! You speak of her as if she had made an unforgiveable mistake."

These words, however, seemed to do nothing to console Lady Hopkins's crumpled spirits. She refused his embrace and stood, tearfully explaining, "You, Phillip, could never understand what it is like to be hunted for your fortune."

Lord Hopkins felt her implied criticism. He sighed, further attempting to soothe her. "But why must you think of that? I did not merely marry you for your fortune, and you can hardly expect a man to find Caroline's fortune more attractive than Caroline herself, can you?"

Lady Hopkins began howling dramatically, her body convulsing with each sob as she returned to the window seat. She grasped a pillow tightly, hiding her face.

Lord Hopkins exhaled deeply and summoned his courage. "Eleanor, are you still upset with me? Have you not punished me long enough?"

Lady Hopkins howled once more. She slowly sat up and blew her nose noisily. "You shall not deceive me any further. I have always tried to be a dutiful wife to you. I loved you quite instantly, as it was, Phillip, but you must own that you used me very badly." She paused to let out a wail. "I found your compliments lost their sweetness and your touch lost its ardency once we were married. Admit it! You married me to save your estate." She was trembling now as she ultimately admitted her fear. "I will not allow my daughters to spend a life such as I have."

Lord Hopkins's heart broke as he listened to his wife's regret of marrying him. He started to speak many times, but felt a loss at how to explain himself. At long last, he blurted, "Perhaps I was attracted to you for your fortune, but that was only at the beginning, and even then, I saw you as the most handsome girl I had ever met, but what followed is quite different. You have always been the most upstanding of wives. You have stood by my side, and I find that I am plagued with guilt—"

"As well you should be!" interjected Lady Hopkins.

"Yes, yes, I know dearest, but you must see that I am in love with you. I have been in love with you ever since the second ball we danced. My guilt has loomed over me these past twenty-six—"

"Twenty-five years," she corrected forcefully.

"Twenty-five years. My guilt has loomed over me these past twenty-five years because I see now that I was so mistaken in courting you simply for your fortune at first. You, yourself, are worth more than any fortune you could have added to my estate. You have rescued a fallen estate, and more importantly, a fallen man. I cannot regret the actions of my youth, for they have brought me my greatest blessing—you, my Eleanor."

Lady Hopkins turned her head to the window, still sobbing.

Lord Hopkins felt his blood begin to boil. His shoulders shook, and he slapped his hand down against the window seat. "Confound it, Eleanor! I have had enough. I have had enough of your moping and self-pity. Have I not given you a life you are proud of? Have we not seen our children grow, along with each other's maturity and capabilities? I will not stand for you to sit here as if your life has been a waste! Has your life been *so* very unfulfilling as that?"

At hearing him raise his voice, Lady Hopkins jumped slightly, shrinking to the corner of the window. Her crying had stopped, but she would not look at him.

Lord Hopkins knew he had unraveled her. "Perhaps I should not speak so, but I cannot contain my feelings on this matter anymore. I did not marry you for your fortune at all. Yes, yes, I know my mother prided herself on her scheming and matchmaking. Her meddling was what brought us together at first, but can you honestly believe I would . . . ," His voice trailed off, awaiting Lady Hopkins's gaze. Her eyes darted up at him and then down again. Lord Hopkins found himself at last kneeling before her. "Do you not wonder why I was late that night, when the sour Cranston was about to declare himself to you?"

Lady Hopkins finally held his gaze.

"I was detained only because of my feelings. I dared not ask for your hand because it was what my mother had schemed, what she had told me I must do. And yet, I found I could not *not* ask because I could not risk losing you forever. I did not wish to deceive you. I would have gladly disclosed my family's financial difficulties if I had been privy to all the unfortunate details. I only knew that if I—"

He was interrupted by a hard slap across the face. His hand instinctively flew to his cheek, the inward sting much greater than anything physical.

Lady Hopkins glared down at him. "How could you not tell me this all these years? I would not have cared then if I had known your situation. I was so in love. It would not have mattered if you were the son of a farmer."

The words had their effect. Lord Hopkins found emotion overcoming him. His eyes filled with tears, and his voice cracked as he explained, "The sting of regret is more than I can bear. There are so many things I should have told you then. I kept thinking if I just showed you, you would know I truly loved you. Alas, it had come to nothing, all my greatest efforts."

In an instant, Lady Hopkins cradled his head into her lap, stroking his hair with her delicate fingertips. Her tender touch, long forgotten to Lord Hopkins, filled him with the greatest sensation. He closed his eyes as she continued stroking his hair, then his cheek. At last, he heard her clear her throat. "Phillip, I am so sorry for shutting you out. I would relive each year with you if I could."

Lord Hopkins sat up, seating himself beside her. He took her hand in his. "It is enough to hear you say so, Eleanor. I only need the rest of your years."

Lady Hopkins let out an incoherent whimper and gave his hand a tight squeeze.

He found himself feeling young again, and all at once, Lord Hopkins carried Lady Hopkins into a close embrace and began kissing her feverishly. At first resistant, Lady Hopkins soon fell into his arms and gave way to his romantic attempts.

"Lucy, I set the book just over here," Caroline explained, making her way to the window.

Lucy was on her tail, when Caroline stumbled backward in a startled fashion. The two sisters were caught in a laughing spell at discovering for the first time their parents in such a passionate kiss.

"Girls, have I taught you nothing?" Lady Hopkins yelled, blushing profusely. "Have I not taught you that a closed door represents a want of privacy, of delicacy?" The reproach resulted in a moment of silence.

All at once, Lord Hopkins and Caroline broke into hysterical laughter. Lord Hopkins began shaking so hard that his face had colored to a dark red, while Caroline had to resort to her handkerchief in order to catch her newly formed tears of laughter. Lucy attempted at seriousness, though her pursed lips threatened a smile. Lady Hopkins eventually gave in, and tears of joy now replaced her tears of sadness.

CHAPTER 34

Caroline had not forgotten Mr. Clark's rejection. She cursed under her breath when she recalled their embrace. It was not a lady's responsibility to declare herself, nor was it considered appropriate. She felt her inferiority to the man on multiple levels. She had been mistaken in his degree of affection for her. At times, she would convince herself he was indeed in love with her, only to be consumed by the memory of his "It will not do." That memory ultimately convinced her of the insufficiency of his feelings. And so it was in mortification that she declared to Lucy that she could not visit Mr. Clark's shop.

"But Caroline, you must! There are simply too many details to be taken into account. Please, I beg you would go pick up my wedding slippers. They should be done, and we have no time to wait for a delivery. I do not understand your refusal. Mr. Clark has always been in your regard, has he not?"

Caroline made an excuse about a headache and the impossibility of her going to town, but when Lucy stood in anger and declared Caroline unfeeling, Caroline found herself confused. "But why can you not send Louisa or another one of our maids to fetch your shoes? I am not in the mood for a chance meeting with Lord Searly. It has been only a month since I refused him, and a meeting would be extremely uncomfortable," Caroline explained.

Lucy's shoulders relaxed. She took Caroline's hand. "I should have thought as much. I am sorry, Caroline. I had not meant to cause you pain. Only, I do not trust Louisa or anyone else's opinion on the matter. My shoes, and every other detail, must simply be perfect. But I would not wish you to be uncomfortable."

Caroline found she could not refuse her sister. Lucy was overwhelmed with the final details of the wedding. The family was set to leave London in a week. With everything that was going on, Caroline decided it was foolish to allow her own embarrassment to dissuade her from assisting her sister at such a time. With trepidation she dressed for town and climbed into the carriage. She resolved that she would not allow Mr. Clark to sense her humiliation. He was, after all, a cordwainer, and she, his customer. There was nothing unusual about their meeting.

The shop entry was empty except for the clerk. He greeted her kindly and offered to inquire about Lucy's shoes. Caroline sat quietly for a few minutes until Mr. Clark followed the clerk from behind the curtain.

Mr. Clark's eyes widened upon seeing Caroline. One hand flew to his hair, brushing out a few specks of wood, while the other hand fell to his apron, smoothing out a wrinkle. "Miss Hopkins, I—" He gave a slight bow, then stood shakily. "I have your sister's slippers."

The clerk handed Caroline the silk slippers.

Caroline examined them, avoiding his gaze. "They are lovely. I am sure she will approve."

The noise of the streets filled the silence.

Mr. Clark cleared his throat. "I have your riding boots nearly finished. Would you like to try them on?"

Caroline was taken by surprise. "My riding boots? I am not sure I know what you are about."

"Yes, the boots your betrothed, I mean—that is, Lord Searly assured me I should have them fitted when they were ready. Did he not tell you? I would have waited for the announcement in the paper, but he assured me it was agreed upon, and I—" Mr. Clark was now looking at the ground.

Caroline gave an uncomfortable laugh. "I am sure there has been a mistake. I have not seen Lord Searly for a month now, and I can assure you there is no engagement between us."

Mr. Clark's face reddened as he almost whispered, "But Lord Searly assured me of the arrangement."

The silence was once more broken by Caroline's uncomfortable laughter. "Lord Searly must have been mistaken. Perhaps he intended them for another young lady."

"Of course. I must be mistaken," he mumbled, shaking his head.

"Yes, thank you. Mr. Clark." Caroline turned to leave, pausing after a few steps. "My family and I are set to leave London in a week. I am grateful for your services and friendship. I wish you well."

"Good day, Miss Hopkins," Mr. Clark quietly replied.

The shock of finding Caroline *not* engaged to Lord Searly stayed with Thomas most of the day. He was only sure of the truth of it when his clerk interrupted his thoughts to announce Lord Searly. Thomas stood instantly, offering his hand.

"Clark, you must know the laugh you gave me," the duke explained as he shook Thomas's outstretched hand. "I received your note by surprise this morning. You see, some fleeting feeling for Miss Hopkins overtook me, but you must know it has come to nothing. I find the girl just as silly as any other." He was laughing now.

Thomas stared silently.

"I will pay you, of course, for your work. I am sure they are an excellent pair of riding boots. But, as you can see, I am quite without a use for them as they were made to the measurements of Miss Hopkins. You must sell them to someone else."

Thomas could not find words to reply. He opened his mouth twice, but found he had no words in such a situation.

"It cannot be disagreeable, Clark," Lord Searly explained, patting him on the back, "I will pay you as promised and you shall make double your assumed price upon selling them!"

Thomas nodded and cleared his throat. "It is a fine arrangement. It is, however, a most uncomfortable situation. You must have read what happened this morning. I give my full apologies, Your Grace."

"It is of no matter, Clark. I am sure Miss Hopkins found it a funny jest. The matter by no means upset her, and I am sure I find no provocation from it. No, rather, I find it all most diverting. You will forgive me, Clark. I will send my man to settle my accounts in the morning."

The two exchanged a few courteous exchanges before Lord Searly left in his carriage.

Thomas held the boots in his hands. He had never made such a pair of ladies' riding boots. He had spent countless hours on the detailing. Lord Searly would pay him handsomely for his work. Perhaps Thomas could sell the boots to another lady. However, try as he might, Thomas could not envision another besides Caroline wearing the boots. He had made them for her. He apprehensively took out a pen and began a letter.

Caroline,
My apologies for this morning.
Please accept these boots, as they were made for you and only you.
Thomas

Caroline felt her heart skip as she pulled out the beautiful riding boots. They were made of black leather and at first glance looked like many of the boots that she had seen other women wear. Upon closer inspection, however, Caroline noticed the intricate detailing. The front of the boot had a delicate floral pattern that swirled around the lip of the boot, cascading down the sides of it. The effect was breathtaking. Caroline ran her fingers over the small carvings, following the pattern to the back of the heel. Inscribed was the letter C. The edges of the C were made into a lovely curve that joined a pair of small flowers. The seams of the boot had been sewed with perfection along a small carved groove that was bordered by an inlay leather of white. Its delicate twists and turns within the black leather looked like nothing Caroline had ever seen.

On the sole of the boot was Mr. Clark's brand. It was a small stamp that read "TJC of London" in script. She ran her fingers across it, tears streaming down her face. She was not wholly aware of why she was crying, only that she felt Mr. Clark had in some way inscribed much more into her boots than his name. She dabbed at her eyes, and looked at the lining of the boot.

There, right before her eyes, was a lining made of pink silk. Caroline blinked in astonishment as she held the boot closer. She began shaking her head in disbelief. The lining of the magnificent riding boot had been sewn with none other than the silk she had been admiring in the market square months ago, the same silk she had dropped on the cobblestone street and the same silk that Mr.

Clark had rushed to retrieve. She breathed deeply as she traced the "C" on the back of the boot, her own initial in the heel. Lord Searly had obviously ordered the boots, but Caroline felt certain that they had never really been from Lord Searly at all.

CHAPTER 35

John had arrived in London just last night, and Caroline hung close to her little brother. He was sixteen now, and was growing at a rapid speed. He had grown an astonishing five inches in the past season. Not only had he grown taller and broader, he had grown in confidence. He begged Caroline to take him to town multiple times a day, but Lady Hopkins forbade it, telling John he was much too young to be affiliated with the ton in any way, lest he fall into gaming or some sort of mischief.

Caroline had spent the days listening to her brother speak of all that had happened in school. John was not a good letter writer, and as diligent as Caroline had been in writing him, it had not had the least impact on John. He enjoyed receiving her letters and did mean to reply to them, but one thing led to another, and he procrastinated his replies for far too long. John had decided it was better to fill Caroline in on all the happenings of school in person. His speech had improved dramatically, and at times, Caroline found herself marveling at the similarities between John and her father. John sounded sophisticated and mature with his new manners he had picked up along the way.

John accompanied Caroline to the park to ride for four straight days before they were to return to Whitefield Hall. Caroline was especially grateful for a ride without her groom, however endearing George was to her, and for a suitable companion that would not protest the logs and fences Caroline chose to jump.

It was not long before the two were racing and competing just as they had always done in Chelmsford. It was after one of these races, that Caroline begged for breath. She dismounted, followed by John, and the two began leading their horses along a broken path of small flowers.

"Well, I will tell you this, *mon petit chou*," John began, "you may have come to London as an elegant young lady ready for courting, but you have not outgrown your boyish ways."

Caroline returned the laugh as she nodded. "Yes, I see you are right, but you cannot fool me with all your talk of school and books. You have certainly not changed, at least not when it comes to character. You are still my favorite brother."

John nudged Caroline with his elbow, replying through his clenched teeth, "And yet, I must be your *least* favorite as well, for I am your *only* brother. I shall not be so abominable as to pretend you are my favorite. Lucy is much more kind to me."

Caroline smirked at this. "I suppose Lucy is much kinder. But then again, John, you will someday see that my teasing has done you good. You would not wish to be all seriousness and little musings. Yes, the more I reflect upon the whole of it, the more convinced I am that I am the perfect sister."

"It is a wonder you have not been married already."

Caroline startled, turning quickly to face her brother. "I suppose you have a reason for saying such a ridiculous comment?"

John laughed heartily and mockingly grabbed her hand. "It is a brother's right to taunt an older sister, though I suppose I would taunt a younger sister if I had one. At any rate, I think only a fool would be immune to you, Caroline. I am your younger brother, and even I see how amusing you are. I have of course, heard of the grand duke's offer. He must have been a capital bore, mind you, but were there not any other attractive offers?" He paused. "You must have had plenty of suitors. Perhaps they were not equal to the task of offering just yet. I am sure you will make a fine match, just as Lucy."

Caroline continued walking quietly. It was only when they neared a large shade tree that she softly explained, "It is not as simple as that, John. I thought it would be, but I find that not all men wish to be amused, at least not the men of character. I will not give up, however. There is one man in London that has caught my eye, and I have determined not to give up on him. There is always next year."

John changed the subject to horses, comparing the town ones to their finest at Whitefield Hall. He began making grand plans for the pair of them while he spent his summer in Chelmsford. In return, Caroline spoke freely about her plans for the summer, demanding that John ride every day with her. Any thoughts of the season had almost escaped her when she felt a set of eyes watching her. She turned and was shocked to see Mr. Clark situated under a nearby tree.

"Thomas—Mr. Clark, I had not seen you. I would not wish to invade your privacy on such a day," she said nervously, turning to leave.

Mr. Clark stood immediately in response, shaking his head. "I am happy to see you. Please, do not leave on my account."

The two parties paused awkwardly, until John offered his hand. "Hello, sir. I am Caroline's brother, John. I recently returned from school for a holiday."

Mr. Clark smiled, his dimple appearing. "I thought as much. I have not often seen such strikingly similar features before." Mr. Clark turned to address Caroline. "You are not wearing the new riding boots. I hope they are to your liking?"

Caroline blushed instantly, but forced herself to meet his gaze. "They are beautiful. Perhaps much more than beautiful. I did not want to dirty them."

Mr. Clark's eyes fell, and he buried his hands in his coat pocket.

She surprised herself by blurting out a lie. "And there was a small matter of fit."

Mr. Clark's head rose, as he scratched his chin. "I would be happy to fix any problem. May I come for a home fitting tomorrow?"

Caroline was assessing Mr. Clark's manner. His eyes were soft and his expression genuine. She caught a hint of admiration in his gaze. "Yes, I think I would like that."

Mr. Clark smiled. "Then I shall call on you tomorrow, Miss Hopkins."

Caroline felt a small seed of hope beginning to blossom in her chest. She turned to John, "We must return home. Mother will be in fits if we are late to tea today. Mr. Frandsen will be there, along with his grandmother. Good day, Mr. Clark."

Mr. Clark grabbed the reins of her horse, and offered his hand as she mounted the mare. She took his hand timidly, but determined to hold her head high. He was now looking up to her tenderly, and she found her feeling of hope rising even more as she turned away and broke into a gallop.

Had John not just returned from school, Caroline would have retired early to bed. She felt the toll of the season and was anxiously anticipating Mr. Clark's company in the morning. But however willing she was to retire, she stayed by John's side that evening, listening as he rattled off stories of school. Caroline found herself leaning in to hear his ramblings. Most of his stories revolved around his strict schoolmasters and the daft schoolboys that accompanied them.

"You cannot imagine the disagreeable man, Caroline! He stood there, with his stick, demanding the answer from poor William. I thought for sure William would turn beet red, but clear as day, he stands up and says, 'Master Flemmings, perhaps if you had taught me better, I could give you the desired answer!' Can you believe it? Flemmings threw him straight out, told him never to come back. But somehow, William found a way back."

Lady Hopkins rolled her eyes, patting John's arm. "Now John, I would not have you associated with such a boy ever again! Your success in life is already determined, and how sad would it be to have your reputation tarnished by such a silly boy?"

John laughed at this, promising his mother it would do no damage.

"But John, you do not know what a slight a reputation can take from such things. Think of your poor sister, Caroline, who—if she would have only accepted the duke's offer, but of course she did not accept it—and, well, John, now she is the gossip of town. How these things get spread about, I will never know. I do, though keenly, feel the blow it must be to you, Caroline," she said, letting out a soft sigh. Lady Hopkins shook her head slowly, her eyes falling to Caroline.

Caroline was quick to reply. "Yes, Mama. I do feel it, but have you not considered that I would be better off without such acquaintances? I do not feel the loss of any of their company. What were they but a few old mothers that had set their own daughters after the duke? No, Mama, I am the better for it." She paused, aware of her mother's intense stare. "And what's more, I think it may do my reputation some good. I would rather be interesting than a complete bore!"

Lady Hopkins fell into a fit of laughter, but not a pleasant one. It was the kind of laughter one does before going into hysterics. After a moment, the laughter transformed into a hacking cough that eventually made its way to exasperated sighs. "What a thing to tell your brother! John, in the future, do not consult with Caroline about any social matters. You must come to me with such things. I will be your guide."

John must have sensed the tension between Caroline and Lady Hopkins for he sat silently, sipping his tea until Lady Hopkins rose to take a turn around the room.

Lord Hopkins entered the room, took a seat next to John and whispered, "What did I miss, my boy?"

John made a subtle gesture toward his mother and then to Caroline, to which Lord Hopkins let out a hearty laugh.

Caroline simply grinned up at her father. "We have been at it again, Papa."

John tilted his head and squinted one eye at Caroline. "Perhaps you should tell her you are only teasing."

Caroline shook her head vigorously. "That would ruin everything."

Lady Hopkins eventually made her way back to the three of them and offered sweetly, "Caroline, I have thought of just the thing! You remember Christopher from Endlesgate? We shall invite him and his family for an extended stay! I am sure you and he would get along nicely. He has, after all, a handsome fortune and is not bad to look at either! I shall write to Ruby and have you married by Christmas, my dear. You will see that all is not lost."

Caroline turned to John, shaking her head in disbelief. "You see, she shall never give up."

Chapter 36

Thomas arrived at the Hopkins' home to find that nearly all the staff had been sent to Whitefield Hall already, except for a butler and one maid. Thomas stood in the front foyer, filled with apprehension, when Lord Hopkins walked by. The baron backed up upon seeing Thomas and gave a friendly gesture.

"Mr. Clark, what a pleasure."

"Lord Hopkins, how do you do? I seem to have come at a most inconvenient time. Shall I return later?"

Lord Hopkins swatted his hand at this. "No, by Job, you have come at the *most* convenient time, for Lady Hopkins, Lucy, and most of the staff are away! The staff has returned to Whitefield Hall, you see—Lucy's wedding—but Lady Hopkins and Lucy are out and about this morning."

Thomas offered a polite laugh, but failed to see a fitting response.

"Mr. Clark, what brings you to my home?" Lord Hopkins said with a smile.

"Lord Hopkins," Thomas began, "I am here for a fitting for Miss Caroline Hopkins. Your butler has gone to fetch her now."

Lord Hopkins nodded, shaking his head with a smile. "I see. I suppose my girl is off to spending more of my money!" It was silent for a moment. "I suppose I should say it bothers me not. It is not my money after all, not rightfully on any account. You see, Clark, I have finally come to terms with it all. I was nearly penniless when I married Lady Hopkins, and you see how she has blessed me—given me all that you see here and one hundred times more."

Thomas was once again caught off guard, and attempted to regain his composure at being taken into the confidence of the baron. "But you had your title, of course. You offered her station."

Lord Hopkins shook his head furiously at the mention of station. "I will not hear of station. If I have ever heard of such a preposterous notion as station! You must forgive me, Clark, but unlike Lady Hopkins, I could give fiddle for the title. I am sure you hear the gossip in town of my Caroline. She has been ousted from much of the ton for refusing the duke! I myself have never been more proud of the girl. She is brighter and has more gumption than most men of the ton. She will not be induced by station, and she will be the better for it."

Thomas smiled, reflecting on the similarities between the baron and Caroline. Not only did the father and daughter look alike, but there was also a resemblance in character, opinions, and boldness. Lord Hopkins cleared his throat, interrupting Thomas's thoughts.

Caroline was descending the stairs. She wore a simple white frock, but there was no mistaking any part of Caroline as simple. Lord Hopkins seemed to catch the admiring look in Thomas's eye as he smiled warmly and offered a small wink toward Thomas. "I shall leave you to your fitting."

The two stood at the base of the stairs for quite some time, eyeing one another. Thomas had not been alone with Caroline since their last meeting in the parlor.

She gave a small laugh. "I suppose we should start the fitting, Mr. Clark?" she asked, gesturing toward the small sitting room.

Thomas nodded. The two were silent as she sat and lifted the skirt of her dress just enough for him to slip on the boot and fasten it. He felt around the boot, squeezing and pinching her foot in places, attempting to discover his error, but he could find nothing.

"Will you show me where it causes you such discomfort?" he asked.

Caroline pulled at the strings, pointing toward the lining. Her eyes fell, and her cheeks turned pink. "Perhaps you can tell me why you lined my riding boots in such finery?"

Thomas swallowed hard. Small beads of sweat began glistening against his forehead. "Lord Searly assured me everything should be first rate."

Caroline's lip curled upwards as she continued to prod him. "And was it Lord Searly that designed such intricacies and the inlay of leather? I have never seen such beauty in a riding boot."

Thomas, now darkened to a deep blush, only nodded. He had inwardly hoped that she would see his effort, but he had never supposed she would humiliate him for it.

"It is strange, Mr. Clark, but I could have sworn I had seen this silk before. Perhaps at the merchant square?" When Thomas said nothing, she only pushed onward. "No, I suppose it is a different silk than what I had in mind."

Thomas stood, dropping her foot. He could not brush off the irritation he felt. "Is this your complaint? The lining is finery?"

"It is not a complaint. I was simply curious."

"Why you would have me come to fit a boot without the least error is beyond me. Miss Hopkins, I shall take my leave, and endeavor to wish you well."

Caroline smiled at this, seemingly satisfied. "In a few days we shall be gone. It matters not. My mother is determined to marry me off to some other connection."

Mr. Clark stopped instinctively, turning to her seriously. "And you would be married to whom she directs you to marry?"

Caroline's green eyes threatened laughter, and Thomas saw she was not about to contradict him. "I would never do anything I did not wish to do."

Thomas shook his head. "I did not think you were so easily persuaded, though I doubt you will ever have to do anything against your wishes. Those of privilege hardly do."

His back was now turned toward her. The silence seemed to swallow them both. Thomas suspected he had injured her, but when he at last turned toward her, he saw she was not affected by his words.

She stood, instead, a few feet away, a playful glisten dancing across her eyes. "And what of my wishes?" she said tauntingly. "You seem to take interest in my wishes, do you not?"

Thomas found his pulse quickening as he began to step backward. He straightened his coat. "I only meant that I would be sad to see you unhappy."

Caroline raised an eyebrow. "But you do not wish to see me happy?"

Thomas's face was now clouded in confusion. He bit the side of his cheek, and then raised his arms. "I've lost your meaning. Of course I wish to see you happy!"

"Then why do you refuse my affection? You allowed me to attach myself to you in every way I could without the prospect of anything lasting. You teased me with possibilities. Yet you refuse to even acknowledge you have caused me pain."

"Caused you pain? Do you think I have not suffered? Caroline, I have come to—" He sighed loudly as he let the words slip from his mouth, "I have come to love you. It is for your own happiness that I have refrained from any further advances. Why did you not, for your own good, forget me and accept the duke's proposal?"

She stepped forward, raising one hand to his jaw, placing the other to the lapel of his coat. She stared at him directly and whispered, "I love you, Thomas Clark."

Thomas's brows furrowed, his dark eyes filled with concern, but he did not stir. She rose to the tips of her toes and placed a soft kiss upon his lips. She pulled back, staring into his dark eyes. In a moment of haze, Thomas found himself pulling her back into his embrace, kissing her quite forcefully on the lips. At last, he released her from his embrace, and shook his head gently. There was no denying it any longer. He could not stand to ever lose her.

Caroline sighed as she pulled her hand away and touched one of his dark curls that had fallen across his face. "It was your dark curly hair and handsome eyes that first stole away my heart. Then there was your character. But, who could have withstood such a singing voice and such dancing?" She let out a small laugh, and then abruptly became serious once more. "I have never known a better man. And for that, I know I am dreadfully unequal. I hope you will give me a chance to prove myself to you. Will you allow me to try?"

Thomas began to laugh in disbelief. "Are you offering for me then?"

"Of course not. No lady of standing would do such a thing. I am only asking you to offer for me," she said as she pulled him behind the curtain. "And, perhaps, to sing to me again."

Thomas found himself behind drapes once more, but this time there was no Charles Jasper to disturb them. Caroline only smiled up at him, her hand in his.

"Caroline," he said, at last at ease. "I cannot promise everything, but I promise you my heart."

She nodded, exhaling softly as she smiled. "I am glad to hear you say it, for there is nothing more I could hope for."

Suddenly, the drape was forcefully pulled back. To Thomas's horror, there stood an angry Lady Hopkins, followed by a blushing Lucy, a grinning John, and a seemingly pleased Lord Hopkins.

"Caroline! How could you?" Lady Hopkins asked. "Do you wish to be both compromised *and* a topic of gossip?"

The only reply Lady Hopkins received was the footsteps of Lord Hopkins as he approached the pair and set his arm heavily against Thomas's shoulder while he grasped the other in a firm handshake.

"So, I was right, then, in assuming that you are in love with my Caroline."

Chapter 37

Lord Hopkins leaned over his desk, a smile on his lips. "You mean to marry her?"

Thomas nodded his head reassuringly. "I only hope that I will not be too much of a disappointment. I have tried to forget my feelings for Caroline, but it is to no avail." He paused, considering his words carefully. "I did try to discourage her attentions. It was not my intention to persuade her into my affections."

At this, Lord Hopkins laughed aloud, shaking a finger at Thomas. "Thomas, my boy, if you should know anything about my Caroline, let it be this: You cannot discourage her from anything she sets her mind to. She is, unequivocally, incapable of being schemed upon."

A broad grin spread across Thomas's face as he nodded in agreement. "So I have seen."

"It is not always a bad thing," Lord Hopkins offered. "Fortunately, she is careful in her ambition and decisions." He stopped, hesitating. "She would not love you, for instance, if she were not wholly convinced of your goodness."

Thomas swallowed uncomfortably at this, turning toward the closed door. His voice cracked as he inquired, "Will it be difficult to gain Lady Hopkins's favor?"

Lord Hopkins fiddled with a few trinkets on his desk. "I suppose she may prove difficult, but, if you are wise and up-front with her about your true feelings and intentions for Caroline, she will discover your good qualities just as Caroline did. Her only concern is for our daughter's happiness. She must know you love her and that you do not wish for only the fortune."

Thomas shot up at the mention of fortune. "Lord Hopkins, I beg your pardon, but I could never with a clear conscience have any part of Caroline's inheritance. You must persuade her to give it up. I will provide." He stopped upon seeing the gleam in Lord Hopkins's eyes. "Please, sir. It is a matter of great pride."

Lord Hopkins stood, motioning for Thomas to do the same. "I understand quite clearly your objections, but may I also make one thing clear? Caroline has a certain pride of her own and as it is her fortune, I am sure she will wish to do with it as she will."

Thomas sighed as his shoulders lowered in resignation. "And so begins my life with the only person with a will as strong as my own."

Lord Hopkins placed his arms upon Thomas's shoulders. "You deserve each other."

Lady Hopkins, at first shocked by the impropriety of the matter and then infuriated at the idea of Caroline marrying a tradesman, sat unmoved by Caroline's words. Her daughter had attempted to explain the details of their unintentional courtship. Lady Hopkins, upon seeing her daughter's mind quite made up, only nodded stoically. To refuse a duke and accept a shoemaker seemed absurd in every way. It was only when Mr. Clark took Lady Hopkins aside and humbly explained his affection for her daughter that she felt anything. And what she felt surprised her exceedingly. For behind his dark eyes and genuine face, Lady Hopkins saw the future of her daughter's happiness. It would take time for her to fully accept him, but she was grateful his intentions were honest.

The family was set to leave in just two days. The complications of Caroline's engagement had left Lady Hopkins in a dizzy spell. Lord Hopkins and Mr. Clark had sat together for some time deciding what action should take place. It was decided that Mr. Clark would follow the family to Whitefield Hall, closing his shop for the whole of two weeks, where Mr. Clark's and Caroline's own wedding details would be determined after Lucy's wedding.

Lady Hopkins was needed at home. The servants endeavored to please her, and she felt her presence had been exceedingly missed. The season had not been without its hardships, but she had, upon further reflection, successfully secured offers for both Lucy and Caroline. Perhaps it was good that Caroline would be married shortly after Lucy. She now had the time to devote to Phillip John.

Lady Hopkins smiled as she pondered her charming son. He had always shown the greatest of promise, much more than those silly sisters of his. And yet, Lady Hopkins admitted she had been too blind to see it before. With his sharp mind and handsome face, she was sure he would secure an abominably advantageous match in the future. For after all, Phillip John favored his father so very much.

Book Questions

1. How might Caroline's life be different if she married Lord Searly? Could she have been happy with him in the end?

2. Was Thomas's reluctance to pursue Caroline a reflection of his regard for her, his own pride, or a mixture of the two?

3. Lord and Lady Hopkins' marriage was very strained for most of the story. Did you think one of them was more at fault for the way things had become? What does their story teach readers?

4. The book is titled *The Second Season.* Besides being a second season for Caroline, in what ways do multiple characters get second chances or seasons of life?

5. Lady Hopkins seemed to change her tone and outlook by the end of the book. Explain the irony of this change.

6. Do you think Lord Searly really loved Caroline, or were his efforts made only out of selfishness?

7. In what ways do the weaknesses and strengths of Caroline and Thomas complement one another?

8. How is Caroline different than other women of the regency period? How do you think she compares to women of today?

Acknowledgments

There are many people that have helped this book along, in one way or another. I would like to specifically thank my editors, Emma Parker and Jessica Romrell, for believing in my book and helping me to make it so much better; Michelle Ledezma for designing a gorgeous cover that never seems to get old; Emily Chambers for answering my many, many emails full of questions; the rest of the staff at Cedar Fort for giving me this opportunity; my friends and family for reading my early drafts, offering helpful suggestions, and entertaining my children while I wrote; my great-great-grandparents, the original Caroline and Mr. Clark, for giving me the idea; my sister Melissa for encouraging me from the start and reading my drafts almost as many times as I did; my sister Becky for making me submit my manuscript just one more time; my husband, Mark, for believing in and supporting me, giving suggestions, and being my walking thesaurus; and my children, for reminding me daily of the importance of dreaming.

About the Author

As the youngest of four sisters (and one very tolerant older brother), Heather grew up on a steady diet of chocolate, Jane Austen, *Anne of Green Gables,* Audrey Hepburn, and the other staples of female literature and moviedom. These stories inspired Heather, and she began writing at a young age. After meeting and marrying her husband, Mark, Heather graduated magna cum laude from Brigham Young University and settled down in a small farming community with her husband and four children. In her spare time, Heather enjoys volleyball, piano, the outdoors, and almost anything creative.

0 26575 18847 9